THE BUCKLEY DT
SHORT STORIES.
BOB

THE

DIAGNOSIS

and other

Buckley Doyle

Short Stories

THE

DIAGNOSIS

and other

Buckley Doyle

Short Stories

Robert Donnelly

THE DIAGNOSIS and other Buckley Doyle Short Stories includes five short stories that were previously available in singular distribution in digital format only. The Diagnosis, The Manuscript, A Problem at the Library, The Mystery Surrounding Agnes, The Howl in the Night, plus two additional stories; Winters Death Room and A Package at the Door, are now exclusively included in THE DIAGNOSIS and other Buckley Doyle Short Stories and are available in both digital and paperback form.

Buckley Doyle Mysteries

Buckley Doyle is a Professor of pre-twentieth century literature at an Ivy League University located in Providence, Rhode Island. In addition to his academic career, Buckley has a passion for solving crimes and mysteries that elude his contemporaries. In this series of adventures, Buckley is faced with mind-boggling and complexing mysteries.

With Love

to

my wife, Deborah

Thank You

for all the help and support

that made this book possible

TABLE OF CONTENTS

THE

DIAGNOSIS

CHAPTER I

"Yes, I'm Buckley Doyle. How may I help you?"

"Professor Doyle, a mutual friend suggested that I show this to you."

The well dressed man standing in front of me reached into the breast pocket of his suit jacket, pulled out an envelope and held it out to me. As I went to retrieve it from him, a look of apprehension came across his face and his grasp grew tighter.

"You'll have to let go if you want me to read it."

I watched as the apprehension within him seemed to increase. Then as he eased up somewhat, I extended my hand and waited for him to relinquish what he had brought for me to see.

After reading the contents of the envelope, I returned it to him and said, "You do realize that I'm a simple college professor, not a private detective?"

"From what I've been told, Mr. Doyle, you're anything but simple."

"As with you, Mr. Anderson."

"So then, you know who I am."

"Yes, and based on the content of this note, I suggest that you contact the police posthaste."

There was no hesitation in Anderson's voice when he answered, "I can't do that."

The two of us remained silent for what seemed like an eternity. For reasons that I wish not to explain, I reached my hand out, took the envelope back and read its contents one more time. Before returning it to him I examined the paper on which the single sentence was written in cursive. After looking at its front, back and edges, I motioned for him to sit down.

Holding the note up to the light, I noticed the watermark, along with the fact that the author used a fountain pen and was left handed. I also detected that the script was hastily applied to the wrong side of the expensive stationery. I held it to my nose for a moment, then handed it back to him.

Anderson stuffed everything into his jacket pocket and said, "Then you'll help me?"

I looked him in the eyes and replied, "I'll give it some thought, Mr. Anderson. As interested as I may be, I have a few questions that I need answered first."

"Certainly, Mr. Doyle, ask what ever you wish."

"Exactly what makes you believe there's anything that I can do to help you?" Before he could answer, I added, "And why is it that you won't involve the police?"

"May I call you Buckley?"

I shook my head slightly and answered, "No." After an awkward moment on his part, I continued with, "Mr. Anderson, perhaps you could answer my questions."

"My doctor told me where to find you. He said he was certain you could help me."

Wanting to clarify a point, I stated, "I suppose your doctor is John Cooper."

"Yes, Dr. Cooper told me that you and he were very close, and if I mentioned his name…"

I cut him off mid-sentence and asked, "Exactly what was it that he said I could do for you?"

"Save my life."

"From the person who's is in the process of murdering you, I presume."

"Yes."

I watched as a hollow expression fell over Anderson's face, and then I said, "You can't go to the police because you recognized the handwriting."

"It's my wife's."

Anderson went silent. When he resumed talking, there was a noticeable crack in his voice. He said, "She passed away a year ago, last November."

"Meet me at my home at 928 Benefit Street tomorrow at 10:00 a.m. I'll let you know then if I've decided to help you or not."

CHAPTER II

After Mr. Anderson and I parted ways, I contacted my favorite grad student and made arrangements for her to cover my afternoon lecture. With that matter taken care of, I found my way across town to pay a visit to the good doctor.

As usual, Dr. Cooper's waiting room was packed. I cut the line at the receptionist's window, pointed at the adjacent door and said, "I need to see John for a moment."

"He's seeing a patient."

I smiled and said, "I'm sure neither of them will mind."

"You can't go in there right now, Mr. Doyle."

I gave John's receptionist a slight wave, opened the door and barged in.

A patient dressed in a johnny turned and looked at me in astonishment as I said, "John, I need to talk to you right now."

"Now is not the time, Buck. I'm sure even you understand the sanctity of an examination room."

"Yes, yes, yes, I'm aware of all that doctor patient confidentiality stuff. However, there are questions that I need answered."

John looked at me with daggers in his eyes and said, "Get... out... now."

"Your office, in two minutes." Then I looked at his patient and said, "This matter is much more important than your health. I'm sure you understand."

A horrified look fell over the patients face as he turned and looked at his doctor.

In an aggravated voice John said, "Out!"

After pacing back and forth in John's office for what seemed like an eternity, I plopped down in his chair and rearranged everything on his desk so that it was more to my liking.

Bored, I stood up and continued to pace. Becoming impatient, I returned to the exam room, opened the door a crack and said, "For god's sake, John, just give the poor bastard a couple of aspirins and tell him to call you in the morning. Better still, have him call you in a couple of days. I do believe we'll be tied up tomorrow."

As John pushed the door shut in my face, I heard him say, "Pay no attention to that man, Mr. Rand, he's really harmless."

Despite all my efforts, the good doctor took his sweet time.

When John walked into his office, the first thing he said was, "Get... the hell out of my chair." Once seated, he moved everything on his desk back to its original position, and added, "What, in all that is holy, was that all about?"

"Mr. Rand is fine."

"He has kidney stones."

"He'll pass them."

"I'm assuming that you're here about Mr. Anderson."

With a smile on my face, I said, "I've decided that we'll take the case."

"What case? And what is this 'we'll' crap, Kemosabe."

"You know damn well what I'm talking about. Poison, death threat, wife coming back from the grave." I paused for effect and then finished with, "Right up our alley, John. Right up our alley."

CHAPTER III

While John tended to the remainder of his patients, I spent the rest of the afternoon in his office pawing through Mr. Anderson's medical records. Unethical, but if we were going to help this man with his problem it was necessary that I learn everything there was to know about him. Doctor patient confidentiality was not my concern. I was not there for that, so I felt that in this situation it didn't apply to me. Therefore, I examined every record that John had compiled regarding Mr. Anderson.

When John finished with his last patient of the day, the two of us caught a cab to my favorite restaurant on Federal Hill. We discussed poison over glasses of wine and plates of tortellini.

While swirling the contents of my glass, I said, "Tell me why you came up with the diagnosis of poisoning."

"I didn't at first." John took a sip from his glass, then added, "Anderson came to me about six weeks ago complaining of a headache, earache and sore throat. A headache that just wouldn't go away was his main complaint along with dizziness."

"It was five weeks ago to be exact, but go on."

"He was also feeling lethargic. I examined him and noticed that he had a yellowish tint to his eyes. I did blood work which indicated that he had an infection. I prescribed an antibiotic and a low dose of an antidepressant."

"Why?"

"Why, what?"

I rearranged the thoughts running around in my mind and then said, "You put him on an antidepressant, most likely Zoloft, because you thought that he was depressed over his wife's death. I can understand that, but you were wrong."

John took a deep breath and said, "Yes, I think I did misdiagnosed him."

"Anderson was back in your office a week later with worsening symptoms. However, at that time you already had the complete results of his blood work, correct?"

"Yes, you're exactly right, as usual. But then again, you already read that in his chart."

I rested my chin on my fingers and said, "Continue. What did the blood work tell you?"

"You already know the answer, so why do you ask me?"

"Yes, but I want to hear you say it."

John gave me the finger and said, "His liver enzymes were way off and his white count was extremely elevated."

"In other words?"

"I suspected that he was somehow being poisoned. So I ordered additional blood work. The results came back inconclusive."

"Yes, I figured that much from when I met with him this morning."

Shaking his head, John said, "So you knew all of this by meeting the man just one time? Pray tell so that I may become enlightened."

"Since you insist. Anderson is naturally pale, but he had a gray hue to his skin. The sclera of his eyes are tinged yellow which most likely are due to his health issues. His eyes were deep in their sockets and surrounded by dark circles. His gait was unsteady. In addition, there was a distinctive odor on his hands."

"You fingerprinted him?"

"Of course not, don't be silly. He fingerprinted himself when he passed me the note from his wife."

John took a bite of his pasta and said, "I should have his latest toxicology reports by mid morning."

"No need. The poison of choice was hemlock."

John chuckled slightly and replied, "A bit theatrical wouldn't you say."

We finished our evening over a glass of cognac. Then John caught a cab home to his wife, and I walked back to 928 Benefit Street.

CHAPTER IV

It was already daylight before I noticed the time. I had spent the entire night figuring out what I needed to know about Mr. Anderson. At this point, my due diligence was complete and nothing about him eluded me. I felt confident.

Besides the fact that someone wanted him dead, my new client was like an open book. Born in England, middle class based on the clarity of his diction, he immigrated here when he was in his late teens. Along with his father and older brother, they started a small used car business. There was no mention of a mother. After a stint in the military, Anderson attended Brown University where he met his wife. After graduating with a degree in business management, he took control of his family's fledgling business and grew it into a massive automotive sales empire. When his father passed, Anderson bought his brother out.

He and his wife had three children; two girls and one boy, all of who continue to work in the family business.

His wife, Charlotte, the pilot and only passenger aboard her small private plane died in a fiery crash as she was attempting to take off from North Central Airport in bad weather.

A quick call to a doctor friend at the state ME's office revealed one more fact about Charlotte Anderson that I found most interesting.

What my research didn't tell me was what Mr. Anderson's exact net worth was, or that of his empire. Based on speculation it is believed that his alone to be around two-and-one-half billion dollars.

I was rubbing my eyes when John walked into my library. I looked up after a few moments to observe him shaking his head, holding two cups of coffee.

"Long night, Buck?"

"Oh, good, you're here. I assume one of those is mine?"

As John handed me one of the coffees he said, "You're wearing the same clothes that you had on yesterday."

"What time is it?"

"9:20"

I smiled and replied, "AM, correct?"

"Yes, Buckley. AM."

I can always tell when John is annoyed with me by his choice of how he addresses me. Buck, if I'm in good standing. Buckley, if he's upset. Of course, if I've managed to totally piss him off, he reverts to using my last name. I, on the other hand, always address him as John, no matter the circumstances.

"Good then, I have enough time to shower and change into something fresh." I stopped at the doorway, looked back at John and added, "Don't let our guest into the library until I've returned."

"I wouldn't think of it."

I was feeling refreshed and sitting in my chair sipping on my strong coffee by the time Anderson announced his arrival at 928 Benefit Street, by pounding on the front door with the knocker.

I looked at my watch. It was precisely 10:00 a.m., I thought to myself, "Business prompt, exactly as I expected."

I nodded to John and said, "Show him in."

John went to the front door without saying a word. When he opened it, I heard Anderson say, "Doctor Cooper... this is a surprise. Is Mr. Doyle here?"

"Yes, please come in. Professor Doyle is waiting for us to join him in the library."

I stood up and greeted our guest. I then pointed to a sofa which was centered adjacent to the opposing chairs that John and I regularly occupy, and said, "Mr. Anderson, please... have a seat."

Before sitting, Anderson said, "I was expecting to meet with you in private."

"I assure you, anything that I say to you, or you to me, can be said in front of Doctor Cooper. Not only is he my confidant, but he is your doctor." Pausing for a moment, I then added, "So if we are to proceed with this matter, be it with the knowledge that the Doctor Cooper will be a full participant." I looked directly at Anderson and asked, " Do you agree with these terms?"

"Agreed."

"Very well then, let's get started." I crossed my legs and asked, "How long had your wife piloted her own aircraft?"

With a puzzled look, Anderson replied, "I don't understand how that question is relevant."

"If we're to get to the bottom of your situation, it is imperative that you be forthcoming with your answers to my questions."

"Fifteen years."

"So is it safe to say she was a proficient pilot?" asked John.

"Extremely."

Without looking directly at Anderson, I asked, "How long ago was she diagnosed with stage four liver cancer?"

Anderson didn't respond. With just a glance out of the corner of my eye to observe his demeanor, I could tell that the answer to my question was too troubling. I sensed there was more to Mrs. Anderson's death than the accounts of the tragedy itself foretold. Not quite sure of the backstory, or even if the facts of how she died lent relevance to the case, I moved on.

"Are you or any of your family members fans of Shakespeare?"

"Yes, my youngest daughter, Amy and I are big fans. I suppose that my married daughter, Sharon, is as well. Although it's me and Amy who often enjoy quizzing one another. But again, I fail to see how your line of questioning will lead anywhere."

"Are your children aware that you're ill?"

"No, I've kept it a secret."

"Perhaps you could arrange for me to meet Amy?" I paused then added, "I have one additional request, Mr. Anderson."

"What would that be, Professor Doyle?"

"I'll need to examine your company's books."

"Again, I don't see how that will aid in your investigation, but if it will, then you have my permission. I trust however, that you will keep that information confidential."

"You have my word, Sir."

CHAPTER V

I dismissed John. Under the pretense of being a friend from Brown University, I accompanied Anderson to his corporate office to meet his family; primarily Amy.

In the conference room I was introduced to Amy as 'Professor Doyle.' Amy was every bit as I had expected. Articulate, business-like, knowledgeable of her trade and possessed a can-do attitude. What I was not expecting, was her appearance. She was petite in stature compared to her father who is a rather large man. She had a certain wholesome look to her, a pleasant voice and I found her easy to talk to. I found myself attracted to her entire being.

"Professor Doyle, how did you and my father meet?"

"In the lounge at the Hill Club. I overheard him reciting verses from Othello."

Amy smiled and said, "That does sound like Dad."

I smiled back at her and said, "I couldn't help myself, so I chimed in."

"So, you're a student of Shakespeare?"

"In a way I suppose, but then again, that's what I do." I paused for a moment and clarified my comment by adding, "I teach Pre-Twentieth Century English Literature."

"I'm impressed."

"Perhaps you'd be interested in attending one of my Shakespearian lectures? As my guest, of course."

"As much as I'd love to, I'm afraid you're talking to the wrong Anderson daughter."

I nodded and replied, "I was under the impression that you and your father enjoyed debating Shakespeare's works."

"To get his attention, yes. But, the real debater, that would be my sister, Sharon. Would you like to meet her?"

"I would like that very much, thank you."

We found Sharon sitting in her office just a short distance from the conference room.

Standing in the open doorway, Amy interrupted her sister and said, "Sharon, I have someone I'd like you to meet. Professor Doyle is a friend of Dad's from Brown." Then she added, "I think you two may have a lot in common."

Before I could say anything, Amy was gone. At first glance I could see that Sharon was more like her father than her sister was. Meticulous in her appearance in every way, she projected an image of being in charge of all she surveyed. The work surface of her desk was clear of clutter, with the exception of a single pad of paper. Glancing down at it, I could clearly see more doodles than words. She was a multitasker.

"Professor Doyle, please come in. Tell me, what is it that brings an old friend of my Dad's to my office?"

"Your father was showing me around and introduced me to Amy."

"I'm sure you found her charming."

"She told me I should talk to you about William Shakespeare."

"Yes, my favorite subject, outside of running this company that is."

I studied the inner workings of her office before I said, "I'm giving a lecture titled 'Shakespeare and His Relevance in the Twenty-First' Century, and Amy said that you might be interested in attending." I watched her facial expression, then added, "As my guest."

"May I bring a guest of my own?"

"By all means. It's at Bates Hall at eight-thirty this evening. The doors open at eight. I'll have reserved seats for you and your guest."

She stood up, shook my hand and said, "Thank you Professor, I look forward to your Shakespeare lecture."

"Be assured, Mrs…"

"Ms. Anderson, I kept my maiden name."

Before Sharon and I finished saying goodbye, a slick dressed man poked his head into her office and said, "Sis, I'm leaving early." He looked at me then added, "I have a meeting across town."

"Brian, I want you meet Professor Doyle, a friend of Dad's."

"Not now Sharon, I'm running late."

I watched as a look of embarrassment overcame her. After a moment of silence, I lied, saying, "I understand, I have a younger brother as well." After a slight pause, I added, "I'll see you this evening."

CHAPTER VI

Before leaving their corporate office, I paid Anderson a visit and informed him that it was imperative for his entire family to attend a dinner party at the Hill Club the next evening. On my way back to 928 Benefit Street, I stopped at John's office. I wanted to be assured that Anderson's treatment plan was well in hand as well as to tell John that it was mandatory he attend the upcoming event.

Once home, I showered and changed into appropriate attire for the evening's presentation. I did a quick review of my notes for the evening's lecture and then walked over to Bates Hall where I waited for 8:30 to arrive. The auditorium was packed and noisy until the lights dimmed. The announcer addressed the audience over the PA system with, "It is with great pleasure that I present Professor Buckley Doyle who will be speaking this evening about one of my favorite people, William Shakespeare."

My hour-long presentation was over before I knew it and concluded with a thunderous applause from all but a few in attendance. Among those not standing was Sharon's guest. I watched him rise and begin putting his hands together only after receiving a nudge from her.

After reaching me in the reception line, Sharon said, "Professor Doyle, I'd like you to meet my husband, Tony."

"I'm glad you could make it on such short notice, and it's a pleasure to meet you, Sir."

31

He replied with, "Nice talk."

I summed him up as an idiot and addressed the remainder of my comments to his wife. After a few frivolous exchanges, I learned all I needed to know about Ms. Anderson and her husband. I excused myself and focused my attention on the next person in line.

That evening I slept well but awoke early and went straight back to my research of the Anderson family. Before I left my home for the day, I made reservations at the Hill Club for dinner for 6:30 that evening. I texted Anderson confirming the time and place and left it to him to make certain that all the participants were in attendance. Then, as part of my investigation, I made a short trip to one of the more shady sections of the city, which was not very far from Anderson's corporate office.

After returning home to freshen up, I made my way over to the club. For everything to go as I have planned, it was important that Hill's staff understood and followed my directions to the letter. I insisted on a private room with actual doors. Also, place cards were to be set out per my seating plan. To ensure success, I asked the Maitre d' to make sure the guests sit only in their assigned seats, with no exceptions whatsoever. Last but not least, the meals were to be served on my command.

I left the dining room, entered the lounge and waited for everyone to arrive as I had expected.

So that I wouldn't be blindsided, John arrived early and we reviewed Anderson's condition one more time. John assured me that I had nothing to worry about with matters concerning our client's health.

"May I get either of you gentlemen a cocktail?" asked the waiter.

"I'll have Pinch on the rocks," replied John. Knowing better, he looked at me and asked, "Anything to drink, Buck?"

"Perhaps later, thank you."

CHAPTER VII

Mr. Anderson arrived at the club alone and before any of his children. With the exception of Sharon and her husband, who showed up together, the remainder of my guests arrived one by one. The fact that they were all on time was a tribute to a well-oiled corporate structure, I suppose.

My plan took into consideration enough time for everyone to consume two or three cocktails. Knowing that I might need his assistance at some point during dinner, I cut John off after his first scotch.

When the timing was right, I had the head waiter announce, "Dinner is served."

As I had expected, my guests were taken aback by the assigned seating. I assured them that this is how it's done at the Hill Club. That calmed their inhibitions and they all sat down in their respective seats.

I, as planned, sat at the end of the table with the door to my right. John sat at the adjacent chair to my left, a fitting location for my lieutenant. Next to John was Sharon and her husband, Tony. On the opposite side of the table, to my right was Brian with Amy next. At the far end of the table, sat their father, Mr. Anderson.

With no one looking my way, I stood up and tapped two or three times on my water glass with my spoon.

Expecting dinner, they got me instead.

34

With the attendees attention focused on me, I started with, "Thank you all for being here tonight. Before we get started, I'd like to take a few moments to clarify a number of points. The first, and perhaps least important, is that I am not a friend, whatsoever, of your father. I never have been and have no intention of becoming one once the remainder of tonight's agenda is addressed."

A quick glance around the table reassured me that, with the exception of Anderson and John, everyone was caught off guard.

Brian covered his mouth and spurted out a mixture of muffled words, hidden behind a phony cough, that we could all detect as, "This is bullshit." Then, clearing his voice, he stood up and added, "I've got better things to do than this."

I stepped somewhat behind his chair and, based on what I'd learned about him on the shady side of town, said, "Feeding your drug habit would be my first guess."

Continuing with his desire not to be a participant in what promised to be a charming evening, Brian stood and said, "I'm out of here."

I responded with, "Sit down, buffoon."

Shocked by my bluntness, Brian sat back down and sunk deep into his chair.

"Let's continue, shall we." After a sip of water, I said, "One of you sitting around this table has made an attempt to murder your father."

After that statement, I had everyone's complete attention. So I cut straight to the facts. With the room in complete silence, I looked at each participant in turn, and added, "He was poisoned. But for those of you who are innocent, and yes, one amongst you is the guilty person, rest assured that his life is no longer in jeopardy thanks to the expert and competent medical treatment provided by Dr. Cooper."

I watched as each of them started looking at one another. Everyone, that is, except Tony. So I started the process of elimination with him.

"Tony, you don't give a damn, do you?"

"Not really," he replied.

"As the company comptroller, you're content with the money you've managed to embezzle over the past five years. What is your tally up to now?" I looked down at my notes for effect and then answered for him, "The results of a quick forensic audit that I reviewed earlier today shows a discrepancy of around ten, possibly twelve million dollars." I paused for a moment, and then concluded with, "You may be a crook with a nasty gambling habit, but Tony, you have no reason whatsoever to be a murderer."

With everyone else mumbling to themselves about Tony's exploits, I turned my attention to my next subject.

"Now we'll come back to you, Brian." With the focus now shifted to him, I eliminated Brian as a suspect with, "You're not a murderer either, son, but you are an addict, hiding behind your father's assumption that you are merely a playboy out sowing his oats."

I looked at his dad and said, "Mr. Anderson, it's time to place your boy into a rehab program and stop feeding his addiction." Letting my comment sink in, I added, "I've made the proper arrangements at two such facilities." I finished with, "I'll leave it up to you to select the best one for your son."

Brian buried his head in his hands as his father looked away from him and said nothing.

With the two men eliminated, I said, "Sharon, that brings us to you. You've worked hard over the years to get to where you are, Vice President of the region's largest automotive sales empire. The only step left is becoming President yourself. So it may seem to an outsider that you, my dear Sharon, would have the most to gain by the passing of your father."

A sly smile came across Sharon's face and then she replied, "You're out of your mind, Mr. Doyle."

"Perhaps, but that's a debate for another place and time. Right now Sharon, we are in the midst discussing your potential as the would-be murderer."

Sharon repositioned herself in her chair and gave me a look that could kill. Pleased with her response thus far, I continued with, "You were your mother's favorite, correct? Nothing to be ashamed about. Quite often the first born ascends to the top of the pecking order while the middle child is mostly pushed aside and the youngest gets the focus of all the attention. Of course, in this case, that particular offspring was a boy. And thus, in your father's eyes the heir-apparent of all he had slaved to build should rightfully be his son. But, thanks to your mother, you, my dear Sharon, have clearly risen to the top."

The quietness of my guests told me I'd hit a nerve. Taking another sip of water, I continued directing my comments to Sharon, "Prior to your mother's tragic demise, she confided in you that she was terminally ill; did she not?"

Sharon responded with a simple nod.

"Like yourself, your mother was an avid admirer of all things, Shakespeare. Wouldn't you say?"

Another nod from Sharon, followed by, "Yes."

"And, why don't you enlighten us as to her favorite play."

"Henry V."

I took a stab in the dark, and said, "And the note she gave you on the morning of the fatal plane crash, what did that say?"

"I'll not die the death of Falstaff."

"According to Henry V, Act 2, Scene 3, Falstaff's demise was described as a slow and painful death. But you, and only you at the time, knew what she was saying. Am I correct or not?"

"Yes. My mother did not want to endure prolonged suffering. So instead… she committed suicide."

"And by keeping the note to yourself you were, indeed, the only person who knew the truth."

Without a tear in her eyes, Sharon replied, "Yes, it was my secret to keep."

"You have my sympathy."

I paused for a moment to allow everyone to regain their composure, then turned to John. "Doctor Cooper, perhaps you could share with everyone, the substance with which Mr. Anderson was poisoned."

"It was hemlock. The same poisonous substance attributed to the death of Falstaff."

"And Socrates, before him, I might add." Looking her way, I said, "Tell me, Amy. How many hemlock trees and herbs do you have on your property? Never mind, you don't need to answer that. It was a trick question. However, I've accounted for no less then twelve such trees or bushes evenly distributed over everyone's property, except yours."

As smile came across her face before I added, "Not so fast, Amy. You're still one of three sitting around this table who can quote Shakespeare. So you're not off the hook, by any means. As a matter of fact, you, oddly enough, are the one person who has the most to gain by your father's death." I went on to explain, "By law, all deaths of otherwise healthy persons require an autopsy. Of course you already knew that. The results would undoubtedly show hemlock poisoning as the cause. Naturally, all fingers would point directly at Sharon, and rightfully so. She possesses the perfect motive. With good old dad out of the way, she'd advance that final step up to the corner office. There would be no one in her way, not her addict baby brother, and certainly not her pretty, younger sister with no ambitions of her own and nothing to gain. But we know better, don't we, Amy. You want to run this company as much as Sharon does and every bit as much as your dad wants it to pass his company on to his only son and namesake, Brian. Isn't that right, Mr. Brian Anderson?"

As the focus switched to the opposite end of the table, I said, "Feel free to stop me at any time, Mr. Anderson." There was only silence, so I continued, "Doctor Cooper's original diagnosis was correct. You were depressed over what you thought was the accidental death of your wife. After being prescribed an antidepressant, you found yourself re-energized, and your zest for life returned. That's when you discovered the note to Sharon, the one penned by your wife, and referencing the death of Falstaff. It puzzled you at first, but in time you figured out its true meaning. Feeling betrayed by both your wife and oldest daughter, you set out to seek your revenge on the one of them who is still alive.

"And you Mr. Anderson, did research and concocted a poison from hemlock that you believed after the diagnosis was revealed would point directly to one person and one person only; Sharon."

Before any bickering had a chance to commence, I made eye contact with good old dad and said, "By the way, Mr. Anderson, you may send the balance of my fee to 928 Benefit Street."

CHAPTER VIII

Leaving the entire Anderson family to wallow in their dilemma, John and I left the Hill Club and retired to my library in my home back at 928 Benefit Street.

Savoring a glass of cognac, John asked, "Why did Anderson come to you and not the police?"

"If the police were involved, and the truth exposed, such as it was, Anderson would have faced a criminal investigation. Thinking that he had stacked the deck in his favor, he instead chose to seek out an amateur detective."

"Civil action, do you suppose?"

"Not a chance. Everyone involved would have much too much to lose."

"What about the death threat from Anderson's wife?" asked John.

"Anderson used his wife's stationary and fountain pen to create a well constructed forgery." I replied.

"And you know that, how?"

"As Mr. Anderson wrote out his deposit check for my services, I observed that he was left handed."

"And that told you?"

"That paying attention to penmanship pays off. After all, the note was penned by a lefty. Mrs. Anderson was a righty."

"It's a pity how the lust for power drives people to the point of self destruction."

"Yes, especially when it's coupled with anger and revenge."

With the events of the evening concluded, John went home to his wife. I poured myself another glass of cognac and while swirling it around in my glass, my thoughts turned to Amy.

THE END

THE

MANUSCRIPT

CHAPTER I

"The deckhand tossed a weighted line with equally spaced knots tied along its length, from the side of the boat. He watched as it sank to the bottom of the river. Upon retrieving it he shouted up to the wheelhouse, in a voice that could be heard from bank to bank of the river, 'Mark Twain.' And thus we have the origin of an American original, Samuel Langhorne Clemens. Which we all know by his pen name, Mark Twain."

The remaining hour of my presentation flew by without incident with the only exception being when I was interrupted by the sound of a door slamming shut after a stranger entered the lecture hall.

At the end of my presentation, I gave my students an assignment to write an essay on 'Authors with Obscure Pen Names and Why They Use Them,' then proceeded to collect my belongings.

While I was packing up, a man's voice called out, "Professor Doyle?"

I looked up to see a tall, lanky gentleman, who looked to be in his late sixties, standing before me. My eyes were drawn to the man's head. It was adorned with bushy gray hair with matching eyebrows. In addition to his unique grooming, he was wearing a well worn, brown suit jacket coupled with baggy pants that didn't quite match in color. His shirt had a tinge of yellow to it, and his tie was spotted with whatever he had for yesterday's lunch. At

45

first glance, I formulated that he was most likely a man who was tired of his job and wished he'd retired yesterday. I was left with a feeling that the poor guy just didn't give a shit about anything.

Despite my first impression, I knew that something other than my lecture brought this stranger here. I answered, "Yes, I'm Buckley Doyle. How may I help you?"

Showing a badge, he introduced himself, "Professor, I'm Detective Frank Callahan with the Providence Police Department."

"If you're here to arrest me, Detective, I can assure you that no part of my lecture was plagiarized." I smiled, reached down for the remainder of my notes and stuffed them into my worn leather bag.

"I'm not here to arrest you, Professor."

"Well, that's a relief." I broadened my smile and added, "I certainly wouldn't want to find myself on the wrong side of the law."

"Professor, I would like to ask you a few questions."

"Questions?" I continued to pack more of my lecture material, and when I was finished, said, "Questions about what?"

"Is there someplace private where we can talk?"

Looking around, I replied, "You and I are the only two in this room. It doesn't get much more private than this. So ask away."

"Very well, I'll get right to the point. Yesterday, a man was murdered not far from here."

"I'm afraid you're talking to the wrong man, Detective. I'm not a professor of criminal justice, I teach literature. To be exact, pre-twentieth century literature."

"We found what we think is a manuscript at the crime scene."

"A lot of people write." I looked at my watch, stood up and said, "I'm sure you think that's an important clue, but I'm afraid time is of the essence, and I need to prepare for my afternoon class."

"It was dated 1921 and was signed, Ernest Hemingway. Does that make it any more interesting to you, Professor?"

I took a few moments and processed all I knew about one of the most eccentric authors of recent time. Not sharing what I recalled with Detective Callahan, I replied, "Yes, Detective, I am interested."

I called my grad student, Annie, and made arrangements for her to again cover my afternoon lecture.

CHAPTER II

Not two blocks from the Brown University quadrangle, we stepped out of Detective Callahan's car, ducked under the police tape and walked into the crime scene. As it turned out, it was located just two houses down from my Benefit Street home. With the exception of Mrs. Jones, whose house is all that separates mine and the one that I now found myself entering, I've made a point of not taking the time to know my neighbors. To be honest, the only reason I tolerated the widow next door was because of John Cooper. After showing up at my door one afternoon, holding a casserole dish of what she was passing off as shepherds pie, John let her in. Despite the fact that it was cottage pie, I haven't been able to refuse her since.

Following the detective through the house, I observed everything, including the bloodstained floor in the foyer. Entering the study, Callahan reached into his pocket, pulled out some rubber gloves and stuck his hand out.

Knowing that I'd be handling paper documents, I retrieved a pair of white cotton gloves of my own, put them on and said, "I prefer these, thank you."

He pointed to the table and said, "These are the papers that I was referring to."

"May I?"

"Knock yourself out."

I turned the unbound papers one by one, examining each of them in turn. Getting close to the end, I said, "Detective Callahan, do you have any idea what you have here?"

"They struck me as somewhat relevant, but then again, that's why I asked you here."

"While covering the Lausanne Peace Conference in Switzerland for the Toronto Daily Star in December 1922, Hemingway befriended Lincoln Steffens, a fellow journalist and editor. Impressed with Hemingway's writing, his new friend asked to see more. Hemingway wired his wife, Hadley, who was in Paris, where they were living at the time, to bring him all of his manuscripts. She packed everything she could find into a suitcase. While waiting for the train, she set the suitcase down on the platform and went to purchase a bottle of water. When she returned, her bag was gone."

Scratching his head, Callahan, said, "So, what you're telling me is that this old stack of paper is the real thing?"

"Yes, I am, detective… and they're worth a fortune."

"Well, I'll be damned."

I looked around the room, then asked, "Do you have any idea what poor Mr. Smith did for a living?"

"His business cards indicate that he was an antiques dealer."

"Try having his fingerprints run through Interpol." Having no idea behind the basis of my request, Callahan took too long to reply, so I added, "Step over please." I pointed to a picture on the wall and asked, "Tell me what you see, Detective?"

49

He looked at it for over a minute and then answered, "A nicely framed print?"

"What you see before you, my good detective, is the very reason that you need to contact Interpol."

"So as to not sound like a complete idiot when I call Paris, please tell me exactly what the hell it is that I'm looking at?"

"Here before you is one of two 15th-century pages taken from a prayer book in Turin, Italy twenty-five years ago. The script is in Latin of course and the person in the portrait, which by the way is offset with gold highlights, is Saint Lawrence being slowly roasted to death by the Romans. It dates back to the Middle Ages."

"You're shitting me, right?"

"I'm afraid your murder victim was a bit more than a simple antiques dealer, Detective Callahan. If I'm right, and most of the time I am, Mr. Smith's main source of income came from the purchase and sale of stolen antiquities."

CHAPTER III

I met my best, and sometimes only friend, John, and his wife Elizabeth, for dinner at my favorite restaurant, Antonio's on Federal Hill, where we discussed murder and antiquities over dinner and a bottle of wine.

As we talked, I detected that I was in the midst of having a split conversation with Mr. and Mrs. Cooper. Every time that I spoke of Smith's murder, John's ears would perk up and he would chime right in. On the other side of the divide however, when I switched the conversation to that of stolen and lost works of art, it was with Liz. To be quite honest, it made for a very spirited evening.

John Cooper and I go back a long time. He was the surgeon who put my leg back together after I was seriously injured by a hit and run driver. During my year of recovery, John somehow managed to track down the driver. By the time I was ambulatory with the aid of a cane, John and I became the best of friends. Over the next ten or so years, John's passion for solving mysteries grew to rival that of mine.

Then Liz entered his life; and over night John's love changed from crime solving to her. But tonight, my allocation of John's attention seemed to grow from a dismal 80/20 split with Liz in the lead, as one would expect, to that of 60/40 with Liz trailing. All I needed to do from there on forward was to make sure that I always involved both of them. And, from what I was observing,

51

that task didn't appear to be difficult given Liz's keen interest in the trafficking of stolen antiquities.

With that thought in mind and no room for dessert, I suggested that we retreat to my place for a glass of cognac and, unbeknownst to either of them, perhaps a little bit of suggestive guidance on how the new corporation of Cooper and Cooper could be of assistance.

Knowing that John wouldn't want to upset his bride by getting involved, I focussed on Liz.

"I have to say, Liz, I'm quite impressed with your knowledge of antiquities."

John gave me a stern look and said, "I know where you're going with this, Buckley."

"John, let Buckley continue."

"I know him too well, Liz. He's trying to sucker me into spending a huge amount of time helping him solve his newest case."

"I'm not a stupid woman, John. I know what your friend is trying to do." Then she turned to me and said, "Go on, Buckley."

"We don't have much time to solve this one. So what I have in mind is the triple divide-and-conquer technique."

"He's using you, Liz."

I smiled at Liz, and said, "John, you're hurting my feelings."

"John and I would love to help. Isn't that right, dear?"

52

John sat there, speechless, as I went on to say, "I'll contact Detective Callahan and arrange for me and Liz to meet him at the Smith residence first thing in the morning." Addressing Liz directly, I said, "While at the crime scene, I'd like you to compile a complete list of the home's inventory of artifacts. Then, once you've returned back here, you can launch an internet search for matches."

"That sounds like a fun day of work."

John smiled with a lack of enthusiasm and said, "And what, pray tell would you like me to do, chauffeur you around looking for clues?"

"Don't be silly, John. While Liz and I are searching for antiquities, you, my dear Doctor, can conduct an interview with my next-door neighbor, Mrs. Jones."

"No. No. No. You can talk to her all by yourself. I'm not doing that. No way."

Liz winked at me, then turned to face her husband, and said, "I'm afraid that's impossible, John."

"And why is that?" questioned John.

"Because Buckley will be with me, dear."

I gave a slight thumbs up and said, "Good then, it's settled."

John just shook his head and rolled his eyes.

CHAPTER IV

By 8:00 a.m., the Coopers were back at my house as planned. With his wife by my side, I wished John good luck as he stood at Mrs. Jones front door. Sensing that John was looking at us, I took Liz's hand in mine and whispered something irrelevant into her ear. Then, as I smiled back at my best friend, I watched John chuck me the finger just as Mrs. Jones opened the door.

"Doctor Cooper; you devil, you," were the only words I heard before she ushered him inside and closed the door behind her.

Liz and I continued on to the Smith house next door. I introduced her as my colleague to Detective Callahan. After familiarizing Liz with a few of the antiquities that I had spotted the day before, I quizzed the good detective about any headway he may have made in the murder aspect of his investigation.

After determining that Callahan and his crime scene investigator friends had failed to produce anything of a tangible nature, I said, "Mrs. Cooper should conclude her cataloging of anything of value by noontime, one at the latest. Shortly thereafter, Detective, I will be able to present you with a full report detailing Mr. Smith's extracurricular activities."

Four hours later, I dropped Liz off at 928 Benefit Street so that she could begin her search on the internet and provide insight into what she had discovered just two buildings away. Leaving her with all she needed to complete the task before her, I went next door to rescue John.

When Mrs. Jones opened the door, I handed my neighbor an unwashed casserole dish from one of her infamous cottage pies and said, "I believe this is yours." I stepped inside and asked, "Is John still here?"

Before she had a chance to answer, John shouted, "I'm in here, Buckley."

As I walked past her, she replied, "He's in the parlor, Professor Doyle."

"Thank you, Mrs. Jones." After turning left into her parlor, I looked at John and asked, "Is this what I'm paying you to do, drink coffee?"

"First of all, it's tea."

"Yes, bayberry tea. Would you like a cup, Professor?"

"No thank you, Mrs. Jones."

"Secondly, I was unaware that you were paying me anything, but now that you brought the subject up..."

"Don't be ridiculous, John. Just tell me what you learned."

After an hour of listening to John being interrupted by Mrs. Jones, and being forced to endure two cups of that dreadful concoction that she passed off as tea, our work there was done.

Understanding the importance of why he was forced to endure Mrs. Jones, but still upset with me, John didn't utter a word as we walked the short distance back to my place.

"Welcome back, you two," As the smile broadened on Liz's face, she kissed John on the cheek and said, "Let me show you boys what I found."

With that, we retreated into my library where John and I were treated to a litany of Liz's findings. I was expecting her to make a connection between lost treasures, but the depth of her investigation amazed me. Clearly, her knowledge of antiquities left me again wondering about Elizabeth Cooper's past life.

I knew that now was not the time to deviate from the present, but I kept hearing that nagging voice in my head saying, "There's something about this woman that I just can't put my finger on."

Not allowing my thoughts to drift, I contacted Detective Callahan and informed him that, in my opinion, we had uncovered substantial evidence pertaining to his investigation. He agreed to meet us at my place at 8:00 p.m.

In the interim, I asked the Cooper's if they would mind walking down to the local deli to pick up some sandwiches. As soon as I heard the door close behind them, I Googled the name, Elizabeth Beck. After expanding my search, I concluded that the surname she had used when John introduced her to me a year ago wasn't hers at all. It appeared to me that John's wife was someone else entirely.

I was still researching the mysterious Liz, if that was even her real first name, when John poked his head through the doorway and said, "Time to eat."

Startled by their early return, I closed the cover on my laptop and was able to force a smile.

"Now, what are you looking up?"

"Nothing earthshaking."

"It's never nothing with you, Buck."

Standing up, I replied, "Let's eat, shall we."

CHAPTER V

Detective Callahan arrived as scheduled. He was accompanied by a colleague of his own, a detective by the name of Paul-Blanc. Unlike Callahan, my initial impression of his associate was that of an ass. Nevertheless, I welcomed them both in and proceeded to my library.

Before getting down to business and addressing my remarks to Callahan, I said, "I don't believe you've ever met Elizabeth's husband, Doctor John Cooper." As John started to extend his hand, I continued the introduction with, "Detectives Callahan and Paul-Blanc, both with the Providence police." After allowing time for ample chit-chat, I added, "Shall we get started?"

"Yes, let's see why Callahan dragged me along with him," replied Paul-Blanc.

"All in due time, Detective." I paused, then added, "But first, perhaps we can all be enlightened as to any progress that the Providence Police have made into Mr. Smith's true identity as well as a plausible motive for his murder."

"Is this guy for real, Callahan?" Asked Paul-Blanc

"I'm the one who approached him for help, and to answer your question; yes."

Paul-Blanc didn't respond, so I turned and asked Callahan, "Have you received any information back from Interpol?"

Callahan answered with, "No, and Detective Paul-Blanc hasn't had much luck canvassing the neighborhood either."

"Perhaps you sent the wrong man."

"No one would answer their doors," replied Paul-Blanc.

"If I were one of my neighbors, I wouldn't answer the door either, Detective. But, I would open it for Doctor Cooper, as did Mrs. Jones next door."

"Then, instead of wasting my time with you, perhaps I should pay a visit to the lady next door."

"I'm sure that she'd be happy to talk to you, if John or I asked her to." Before Paul-Blanc could escape the pissing match, I went on with, "Perhaps I can get started sharing what we learned about Mr. Smith and the extent of his business dealings. But first, let's discuss why he was murdered."

"I think that's a great place to start," replied Callahan. "Go on."

"It appears that the dearly departed Mr. Smith entertained a lady friend precisely at 10:30 a.m. every day except on the weekend. Then as time went by, she added Saturday to her visits. Sunday was the only day that she didn't pay him a visit. Not wanting to raise suspicions, Smith introduced his daily visitor to his neighbor as his housekeeper, Rose. With no available parking spots on the street, Smith asked Mrs. Jones if it would be okay for Rose to park in her driveway. There was no reason for us to believe that the housekeeping thing was anything but the truth."

"So, are you thinking Rose murdered, Mr. Smith?" asked Paul-Blanc.

"No, not at all."

"Would you like to explain, Professor?"

"Although their housekeeping arrangement was exactly that at first, it wasn't long before Rose went from taking care of Mr. Smith's home to taking care of him. Gentlemen, they were not murderer and victim, Rose and Mr. Smith were lovers."

"I didn't see that coming," replied Callahan. Then he added, "Wait a minute, you said they...."

"Yes, there's more. The double murder that took place in Johnston yesterday has a direct connection to the one that occurred two doors down from where we are sitting right now."

"So, what you're telling us is that you think Rose's husband murdered Smith as an act of revenge?"

"Yes, and then he went home and killed his wife. Realizing what he had done, he then committed suicide."

I gave both detectives time to absorb what they had just learned. I then listened intently as they each made a few necessary calls to both the Providence and Johnston police headquarters.

With that aspect completed, I said, "Detectives, let's move on, shall we?"

"There's more?" asked Paul-Blanc.

"Quite a bit, I'm afraid. For starters, Smith was an alias. His real name, from what we've been able to learn, was Eric Miner, a Dutch National who's name is linked worldwide to the disappearance of numerous works of art and antiquities.

"As it turns out, Mr. Miner's, a.k.a. Smith, empire was located right here in Providence. Millions, if not billions, of dollars worth of stolen or otherwise missing treasures were trafficked from right under our collective noses.

"Being able to identify the vast conglomeration of items found in his home after his untimely demise, Elizabeth then cross-referenced the items to an international database. What she discovered was astounding, and unfortunately too vast of an assortment to cover here this evening. I have, however, taken the initiative to prepare a Claim of Discovery List detailing each item, and have submitted it to the International Art Loss Register. I have also made a copy for your report, Detective."

After watching Callahan scan the two page list, I added, "As you can see, Detective, at the bottom of the report, I've requested that all reward compensation be forwarded to Doyle and Associates, 928 Benefit Street."

After scanning the Art Loss Register report, the two detectives left, both with perplexed looks on their faces. Not long after, John and Liz left for the evening. Alone, I walked back into my library and poured myself a glass of cognac. Relaxing in my favorite chair, I stared at the contents of my glass and wondered more about Liz.

THE END

THE PROBLEM

AT

THE LIBRARY

CHAPTER I

Despite the weather, I convinced myself that it was an excellent morning for a walk. Fortunately for me, I had stuffed a few dollar bills as well as some loose change into my pocket before I grabbed my house keys. The further from my house that I walked, the more threatening the skies became. In an attempt to dodge the precipitation, I found the nearest coffee shop and stepped inside. An hour later, after going through every last cent on me, it was still raining and I was questioning the accuracy of my favorite TV weather girl.

With few options at my disposal, I chose between the two best alternatives. Walk all the way back home and become fully drenched or dash to my office in the Brown Faculty Building. Even though it was a mere two blocks away, it was in the opposite direction from my abode. The decision was obvious; the answer was my office. Once there, I could grab my umbrella, raincoat and, of course, my galoshes, all of which hung behind the door for occasions such as this. After becoming well equipped, it could rain all day for all I cared.

When I arrived at my office, I found the front door to the building locked. Then it struck me; it was Saturday and the only access in was through the security office which was two entrances down.

Once inside, I confronted a young security officer with whom I was unfamiliar. Likewise he was unaware of who I was and when he asked to see my ID. I was unable to produce it since I

THE PROBLEM AT THE LIBRARY

forgot my wallet at home. The end result of our impromptu encounter was that he wasn't about to let me pass anywhere beyond his desk, much less go to my office.

As inconvenient as it was, at least I was pleased that this new security guy was doing his job.

I had no choice but to brave the elements and walk home in the torrential rain.

Three quarters of an hour later and completely soaked, I arrived back at the front door of 928 Benefit Street.

Still fidgeting with my keys, I heard a man's voice behind me say, "Professor Doyle?"

I turned and said, "Yes, I'm Buckley Doyle. How may I help you?

Flashing his credentials quicker than I could read them, he said, "I'm Special Agent Anthony Diel with Homeland."

Not paying any particular attention to him and being more interested in getting out of the rain, I replied, "Homeland what?"

"Homeland Security, Professor."

Stepping inside my doorway, I turned and said, "May I have another look at your credentials please?" While he stood there in the pouring rain, I added, "Is the nation under attack or something?"

"No sir."

"Have I been threatened by a homegrown terrorist?"

"No sir, you have not."

Already off to a bad start to the day, I stood there hoping that perhaps he would just go away.

With rain dripping off his face, Agent Diel asked, "May I come in?"

I watched as the rain dripped down his face, I gave his request some consideration, and replied, "If you feel that you must intrude."

"Sir, It's raining."

Without making any eye contact, I waved this soaking wet stranger into my home.

CHAPTER II

"Exactly why is it that I came home in the middle of a horrendous downpour and found Homeland Security waiting for me at my door?"

"We would like to ask your opinion about something."

"If they are questions pertaining to any of my students, then I'll have to refer you to the university's admissions office."

"It's nothing like that, Professor. We need you to look at something, then give us your opinion."

"Can you excuse me for a minute? I need to change out of these wet clothes." I looked at him dripping all over my foyer floor and added, "I'll be right back."

When I returned, I brought a fresh towel with me and handed it to him. Motioning him to follow me, I led Special Agent Diel into my library. As I pointed to the couch, I said, "The towel is for you to sit on."

"Thank you."

Before sitting in my chair, I asked, "Would you like a hot cup of tea, Special Agent Diel?"

"No thank you, Professor."

"Make yourself comfortable, Agent. I'll be back shortly." When I returned, I sat in my chair, took a sip of tea, and said, "Tell me again. What is this all about?"

"The Agency needs you to look at a book and tell us what you can about it."

"That's it?"

"Pretty much."

"Okay then. let's see it."

With a grim expression on his face, Diel said, "I don't actually have the book with me, Professor."

I had that feeling all along. With the exception of perhaps one of my students, I've never been approached by anyone and asked to examine a book, or anything else of value for that matter, that they actually had with them. Usually they're items of historical value and in a place of safe keeping. Most of the time I end up disappointing the owner by telling them that they've been duped, that their prized possession is nothing more than a fraud. But, then again, none of those people have ever sent Homeland Security to fetch me.

"So, Special Agent Diel, if you don't actually have the book with you, then where is it?"

"The Library of Congress."

I chuckled as I responded, "The Library of Congress?" When the moment of my humor passed, I said, "Are you kidding me? I'm not going to Washington to look at some book. I have classes to teach that are flowing over with youngsters who have empty skulls that I need to fill... with important... stuff."

"Professor Doyle, your academic schedule has already been cleared with Doctor Jones at the University."

"I don't care if you cleared it with the goddamn Pope, I'm not going anywhere with you or anyone else."

"Excuse me for a moment, Professor." Then Diel pulled out his phone and called someone that I could only presume was his boss.

Giving him the privacy to vent, I returned to the kitchen to make myself another cup of tea. Not being one to eavesdrop, I was still able to hear a little of his conversation as he explained my reluctance to cooperate with his travel plans. With the whistle on the teapot subsided and a fresh bag steeping in my cup, I walked back into my library.

As soon as I entered the room Diel took the cup and saucer from my hand, spun me around, and as he cuffed me, said, "Buckley Doyle. You are under arrest."

"For what?"

"For interfering with a federal investigation."

"You're kidding; right?"

"No Sir, I am not. You have the right to remain silent. Anything you say may be used against you in a court of law..."

Interrupting him, I protested with, "You can't be serious."

Agent Diel was unfazed and continued reading me my Miranda rights.

CHAPTER III

Three hours later Special Agent Diel removed the cuffs from my now sore wrists. I looked at my watch, it was 4:00 p.m. What had started out as a simple morning walk on my day off, had lead me on an unwanted visit to a strange hotel suite somewhere in the heart of the nation's capital. I looked out the window and glanced across the roof of the Lincoln Memorial all the way down to the Capitol Building. Just behind, and a little off to the right, I could see part of what I could only assume was my true destination; The Library of Congress. Based on my view I concluded that the hotel that I was being held at was just across the Potomac River in Arlington; in all likelihood, the Rosslyn section. I was supposed to meet John and Liz Cooper for an early dinner at Antonio's, my favorite spot on the Hill. To clarify, that's Federal Hill in Providence, Rhode Island, not Capitol Hill in DC. Yet, there I was, becoming increasingly pissed off.

Feeling my pissed off meter starting to peak, my anxiety was interrupted by a knock on the door followed by it's opening. I watched as someone from room service wheeled in a cart, removed the silver domed cover and without so much as a single word exited the room.

I walked over to the cart. There were two meals.

A minute later there was another knock and the door opened for a second time. The well dressed gentleman who walked in said, "Professor Doyle, my name is Jonathan Stapleton. I thought that we could talk over dinner, if that's okay with you?"

71

"Yes, and perhaps we can start by discussing exactly why the nation's Chief Librarian had me kidnapped. I'm sure it wasn't for the purpose of chitchatting about our reading habits. But I digress, please have a seat."

"Thank you, I appreciate your coming down here on such short notice."

"I'd like to say that it's my pleasure but I didn't have a choice in the matter."

"I understand. However, under the circumstances, it seemed to be a prudent measure."

I uncovered my plate, it was tortellini. Knowing that there was no way that it could compare to Antonio's, I picked up my fork anyway and asked, "Just how long have you had me under surveillance?"

"I'm afraid that I can't answer that."

"Then answer this. Why the hell am I here?"

"The Library of Congress has a problem with its Gutenberg Bible."

"Exactly what kind of a problem are we talking about that justifies my kidnapping?"

"We were hoping that you could tell us, Professor." Stapleton took a bite of his dinner and after putting his fork back down, he said, "The Bible seems to have gained weight."

"Perhaps your maintenance staff needs to reduce the setting on your humidification system."

"I assure you Professor, that was the first thing we looked at and it's in perfect working order. No other books or artifacts in the room have been affected whatsoever. The situation is unique only to that one item."

"You do know that I'm just a teacher, right?"

Stapleton looked straight into my eyes and said, "Professor, we know more about you than the simple fact that you like tortellini." He placed his napkin on his plate, stood up and added, "My driver is waiting. Shall we go?"

"But I haven't finished eating."

CHAPTER IV

It was 6:00 p.m. on a Saturday evening. There was no traffic to speak of, and The Library of Congress was closed. Except, of course, for my prearranged private visit. The sporadic hustle and bustle that I had always found to be a distraction during my previous visits to this institution was now replaced by two security guards at the front door and a single librarian sitting at the central helm of the library.

"Good evening, Mr. Stapleton," said the guard who let us in.

Stapleton nodded and replied, "Thank you, Robert." As he swiped his ID card, he added, "Robert, this is Professor Buckley Doyle. If you could assist Mr. Doyle with our guest register I'd appreciate it."

"Certainly, Mr. Stapleton." replied Robert.

Then the guard turned to me and said, "May I see your driver's license, Mr. Doyle?"

"No, you can't, Robert. I'm afraid I left it on my end table when Homeland Security kidnapped me this morning."

"Robert, just sign him in as a personal guest of mine, please."

"Very well, Sir."

While Stapleton and Robert were busy with the security issue at hand, I walked out onto the main floor. While looking up at the book filled mezzanine that encircled the rotunda, a woman's voice said, "Professor Doyle, welcome to The Library of

74

Congress." Bringing my attention back to floor level she added, "Impressive isn't it." Before I could answer her, she continued, "Professor, I'm Jessica Welch."

I shook her hand and replied, "Charmed."

"As am I, Professor."

"You wouldn't by any chance be, J. A. Welch, would you?"

"In the flesh, I'm afraid."

"In that case, I'm very charmed indeed."

Our chitchat abruptly ended when Stapleton joined us and said, "I see you two have already met." Without stopping he added, "This way, Professor Doyle."

I looked at Ms. Welch and asked, "Will you be joining us?" She nodded yes, so I said, "After you, Ms…"

She interrupted me and said, "It's Jessie."

"In that case then, after you, Jessie."

"Thank you, Professor."

A few steps later I leaned forward a little and whispered, "Actually, if we're going to be on a first name basis, then you should call me Buckley."

While continuing to walk, she turned her head back toward me and replied, "I'd like that very much, Buckley."

I smiled, and the three of us passed through a doorway that Stapleton used his ID card to open. We entered a less elaborate area, one that I was sure was off limits to the general public.

As the elevator door opened and we stepped in, Stapleton said, "We've moved the Gutenberg to a secure lab where it can be examined."

I looked at the indicator when I heard the bong announcing the floor arrival. A second later we were in a room two floors below the main gallery. As rooms go, this one appeared sterile. In the center was a separate ten-by-ten glass enclosure which held the Bible I was brought here to see.

As I looked through the glass, Jessie said, "We'll need to gown up before we go in."

"Of course."

Before we entered, Stapleton's phone rang. When he hung up, he said, "You'll have to excuse me Professor, but I need to address this call immediately." Then he turned his attention to Jessie and added, "Don't hesitate to call me for even the slightest problem."

As Jessie and I entered the airlock to the glass enclosure, I pivoted around and watched Stapleton exit the room. I turned forward only to be hit in the face with a blast of air followed by Jessie saying, "Are you coming, Buckley?"

"Does he always run off like that?"

"Never. It must be very important."

I thought to myself, "After dragging me all the way down here, what the hell could be more important than this?" Then, out loud, I asked, "Do you always keep the real Bible down here?"

"No. With the exception of annual inspection and cleaning, our Gutenberg is on public display in the Documents Gallery."

"So what's wrong with it?"

"Somehow it managed to gain eight grams between the time it left the gallery and when I started conducting my pre-examination two days later."

"Where was the bible for the two days since it left the Document Gallery?"

Jessie replied, "Right here in my lab."

Trying to simplify the problem, I said, "Perhaps it absorbed a bit of moisture on the trip down here."

"This particular copy is on velum."

"I know, but the binding and cover isn't. Those materials are absorbent."

Jessie shook her head and said, "That's the first thought that came to my mind, but the cabinet that you see it in now is where the bible lives full time. It has its own self-contained environment control system, with its own emergency battery back up." She paused for a moment and then continued, "When the unit is moved, it's transported in its entirety and is only opened, under my supervision, when it's inside this room."

"How do you know it's gained weight?"

"When I plugged my tablet into the cabinet's microprocessor, it flashed an alarm code that went straight to Dr. Stapleton's computer. So right away he had me run diagnostics of everything

77

and conducted a parameter check to make sure nothing in the system went haywire." She paused and then added, "It was clean." Then Jessie took a deep breath and said, "Of course, I would have done that anyway."

"And the bible itself checked out fine?"

"I couldn't tell you. I was instructed not to proceed until you were here."

"Your boss knows that I'm a professor of pre-twentieth century literature and not a forensic archaeologist; doesn't he?"

"I tried to tell him that."

I looked at her puzzled, and said, "You did?"

Jessie smiled and replied, "Yes. I did my graduate work at Brown. You were one of my professors."

"I was?"

CHAPTER V

It was obvious to me that the first step in solving the mystery of why this particular Gutenberg Bible gained weight, when none of the other forty-eight copies known to exist in the world hadn't, was to open the cabinet. So I looked at Jessie and said, "Shall we?"

Jessie's voice sounded full of apprehension as she said, "I suppose so."

"Okay then. How do we do it?"

"It's password protected." Then she entered an alphanumerical sequence into her tablet that included both upper and lower case letters. When the nine keystrokes were completed, she hit enter.

"That was quite an involved array of characters."

"Jonathan changes the passwords for all the cabinets every two months."

"Jonathan, as in Stapleton?"

As the word 'open' appeared on her tablet, Jessie said, "One and the same."

I stood back and let Jessie open the small access door, then reach inside to each corner and release four concealed latches. She then motioned to me to grab a side. Following her lead we lifted the glass cover off the lower portion of the cabinet and then set it on the table. With the bible exposed, I just stood there wondering what we should do next.

Over the years, I had managed to see a total of eight Gutenberg Bibles, but had never touched one. Putting on a pair of cotton gloves, I turned to Jessie and said, "May I?" Then I reached down and turned a page.

"What do you think?"

"I think I need to turn more pages."

Jessie looked at me and said, "That's not what I mean."

"What then?"

"I mean, doesn't it make the blood rush through your veins?" She smiled and added, "You know; give you goosebumps all over?"

"You mean, like does it send chills down the back of my spine?"

She stood back, turned her whole body towards me, put her hands on her hips and said, "Yes. Exactly like that."

While turning more pages, I replied, "No."

"How on earth can you say that?"

"If you could be quiet for just a minute." I finished what I was doing and said, "Okay. You can continue talking now."

As Jessie babbled on about I don't know what, I removed one glove, put my hand to my mouth and wet the tip of my index finger. As she looked on I then placed a spot of moisture on one of the words.

Shocked, Jessie said, "You can't do that."

"Why is that?"

"Because…"

Finishing Jessie's sentence for her, I said, "Because this particular Gutenberg Bible is a forgery."

"What do you mean, a forgery?"

"The action of producing a copy of a document, signature, or work of art."

"I know what a forgery is, smart ass."

"But yet, you didn't know this was one, did you?"

With a stern look on her face Jessie said, "No. But I'm sure I would have if I'd been given a chance to examine it."

"Which brings up the question. Why weren't you?"

She didn't answer my question, instead saying, "Show me why you say it's a fake."

CHAPTER VI

Before I could tell Jessie why I thought that their copy of the Gutenberg Bible was a forgery, Stapleton burst into the glass enclosure and said, "Professor Doyle, it appears that your services are no longer needed, so I must ask you to leave. And Jessica, we'll be placing the library on lockdown in ten minutes, so I must ask that you leave as well."

Puzzled with the sudden turn of events, I said, "That's it. You drag me down here and just like that you tell me to leave. What's going on?"

"Jessica, would you please see to it that Professor Doyle gets safely to the airport."

Jessie looked at me and said, "Come with me, Professor."

As we were leaving the area, I turned back to see Stapleton turning the pages of the bible. Before I could tell what he was up to, Jessie and I were in the elevator and the door closed. When it opened again we were met by Robert, who immediately escorted us out of the building.

Once outside, I turned to Jessie and said, "What was that all about?"

"I have no idea. That's not like him, he's always so reserved." Then she added, "I'll call you a limousine."

When we reached the corner, I said, "It's been an interesting evening Jessie, but I think I'll just find my way back to the hotel, if it's all the same with you."

Jessie kissed me on the cheek and said, "Take care of yourself, Buckley."

"You as well. Perhaps our paths will cross again someday under better circumstances."

When the light changed, I crossed the street in one direction and Jessie crossed in the opposite direction. I made my way west down Independence Avenue to Jefferson Drive. I figured that a walk along the mall would allow me to refocus my mind and figure out what the hell was actually going on with Stapleton and the bible.

About halfway to 7th Street, I heard my name called. I turned to see Jessica running toward me.

Breaking her stride, but not stopping, she grabbed my by the arm and started to pull me along in the same direction that I was already headed, as she said, "Keep going."

"What?"

When we reached the gardens on the grounds of the Smithsonian Castle, we turned in and ducked behind a row of hedges. She continued to tug my arm as she directed me to hide.

"Will you please tell me what this is all about."

She whispered, "You're being followed." Then Jessie put her finger to her lips, motioning me to be quiet.

For the next few minutes we remained kneeling close to the ground like a couple of school kids hiding from the Truant Officer on an unscheduled day off. Then without a sound, Jessie pointed to a man walking by our hiding spot. It was Robert.

We waited for him to pass. When he didn't return, Jessie and I left the gardens through the back entrance and headed toward a nearby Metro station. Once underground, she led me to the platform for the Orange Line. I looked up at the sign. It read, 'Inbound.'

Not knowing exactly where she was intending to take me, I said, "If we're trying to elude someone, for what ever the reason, wouldn't it make more sense to catch an outbound train?"

"I'm sure that once Robert figures out that he's lost us, the first place he'll most likely look is my place. That would put him on the Orange Line headed out of the District." Jessie paused for a moment, then asked, "So what was it that you found that makes you so sure that our Gutenberg is a fake?" The flashing sign announcing an arriving train caught her eye, and she said, "This one is ours. You can tell me later."

"How well do you know your boss?"

"Apparently not as well as I thought."

CHAPTER VII

"Where exactly are we going?" I asked as the train sped off.

"Georgetown. A friend of mine asked me to water her plants while she and her husband are away. I think this is a good time to start."

"Are either of them coworkers of yours?"

Jessie shook her head and replied, "No. Why?"

"Then it's safe to think that Stapleton and his associate don't know them." Then I asked, "This may sound like a strange question, but do you have any money on you?"

"About sixty dollars, why?"

"Good, because I don't have any and we'll need some to buy a couple of Metro passes so we can get off this train."

"I have a Metro card."

"I'm sure they know that."

I watched the sign on the station wall that read, "Foggy Bottom." As the train eased up to the platform, Jessie stood up and said, "This is our stop."

Before we reached the escalator that would take us up to the street, I asked Jessie if I could borrow her phone. When she gave it to me, I made sure it was turned on. Then as we exited the station, I nonchalantly dropped it into the shopping bag of the first touristy-looking person I saw who was headed in the direction of the District.

When Jessie gave me a look that could kill, I said, "Don't worry. I'll buy you a brand new one."

Once we were out on the street, we headed left and walked towards Jessie's friends place in Georgetown. There seemed to be surveillance cameras located at every corner we passed. For sure they were plastered all over every Metro Station and I was positive that Stapleton would have no problem accessing any, or all of them.

When I put my arm around Jessie and pulled her to my side, she said, "What are you doing?"

"We'll draw less attention as a couple than we would as two individuals looking for a place to hide." She gave me a puzzled look, so I added, "Security cameras everywhere."

She pulled me in tighter and replied, "Oh."

We walked awhile and once in Georgetown, we took a right turn down a narrow side street, and ultimately up a flight of stairs. After fumbling through her purse, Jessie pulled out a set of keys. When the door was unlocked, we went inside and then headed up the common stairwell.

It was your typical third-floor Georgetown flat. Old, nicely appointed and, I was sure, overpriced. Oddly enough though, it was exactly what I thought a safe-house should be. All the elements were there. An unassuming setting, one bedroom, small kitchen, a back staircases and, best of all, a front window from which one could look down at the street below. I thought to myself, "If I were writing some sort of cloak-and-dagger detective novel, this would be the perfect hideout with an excellent view." There was only one problem though; I needed to contact my colleague, John.

With any luck, Stapleton and Robert were hot on the trail of Jessie's phone which I hoped was now in some hotel room, somewhere in the middle of the District.

"Are you by any chance still in possession of your tablet?"

Jessie gave me an apprehensive look and said, "Why?"

"Don't worry, I'll give it back."

"In one piece; right?"

Jessie handed it to me and after I entered an address, I wrote, "George Borne needs cash and a new phone." She looked at what I had written with a puzzled look on her face. I hit send, and said, "It's to my friend, John. He'll know what it means, I hope."

The sleeping arrangements were simple enough, Jessie took the bedroom and I laid down on the couch. Restless, it wasn't long before I was standing at the front window with the curtain pulled back ever so slightly. I couldn't say for sure, but if I were a betting man I'd put my money on the fact that it was Robert standing in the shadows across the street.

I found Jessie's tablet and wrote out a second message. After it was marked delivered, I erased it as I did the previous one.

CHAPTER VIII

The next morning, before Jessie awoke, I rummaged through the apartment and in one of the closets I found what I was looking for. While I was at it I borrowed some clothes. The outfit that I ended up wearing wasn't anything that I would have purchased for myself, but it would do. Besides, it wasn't what I had on yesterday.

Satisfied with all my findings, I grabbed a slip of paper and wrote a note on it, shoved it into my pocket and said, "Time to wake up, Sunshine. We need to get started." After another forty-five minutes I asked, "Are you ready yet?"

Twenty minutes later Jessie walked out of the bedroom looking like a million bucks. The tortoiseshell glasses, along with the pulled back ponytail that had given her that librarian look the previous day were gone. In their place, standing in front of me was a stunning woman wearing an outfit that looked like it was expertly tailored just for her.

We didn't blend together, but I didn't say anything because it didn't matter. My guess was that her girlfriend, who's apartment we had used as our safe house for the night, and Jessie, were the same size.

"Where are we headed?" asked Jessie.

"Our first stop is the Wall."

We caught the commuter trolly back to the Metro station at Foggy Bottom. From there we walked a few blocks south to the Washington Mall and the Vietnam Memorial.

As we passed along the rising black panels of names, Jessie said, "You still haven't told me what you found wrong with the Gutenberg."

"Now is not the time. We need to find George Borne."

Jessie looked around and then replied, "What does he look like?"

"He looks like the rest of the fifty-eight thousand plus names of the honored dead. God rest their souls."

Jessie looked a little uncomfortable with my reply, or perhaps it was simply the surroundings in which I said it. Looking around as though she was standing guard, she remarked, "Why is it we're here again?"

As we walked a little further I replied, "I need to find the correct George Borne and leave him a note."

"There's more than one?"

I ran my fingers down the list of the faceless names that were engraved on the fifth panel from the far end, I said, "There are twenty-five men named George Borne here."

"How do you know which one is his?"

"He was the only PFC Borne who died on 2/11/68." A few names lower I said, "Found him." After wedging the note that I had written back at the Georgetown apartment into the letter 'B' and when I felt confident that the note would stay in place, I turned to Jessie and added, "Done. I'm starving, let's get some breakfast."

"That's it?"

"It is for now anyway. After we finish breakfast, we'll be off to Arlington to meet John."

"Who is this mysterious John fellow, again?"

"You really need to keep up, Jessie. John is a colleague of mine who is, as we speak, on his way to rescue us with money and a new phone."

A little confused by our current chain of events, Jessie said, "Arlington's a big place." Giving it a bit more thought she asked. "Exactly when and where are we supposed to meet this friend of yours?"

I thought of my impending reply for a second and then said, "His name is John Cooper, and as soon as he's finished with what I asked him to do, he'll be joining us at my Uncle John's headstone in Arlington National Cemetery."

CHAPTER IX

After the waitress took our order, I looked at Jessica and said, "I think someone has been substituting fake pages into the Library of Congress' Gutenberg Bible." I gave Jessie a minute, then added, "How well did you say you knew Stapleton?"

"I've always had a bad feeling about that man, and Robert as well." Then Jessie added, "Why do you ask?"

"Because I think someone tipped his or her hand at the moment the library was put on lockdown, and that same person set Robert hot on our asses."

"How could anyone think that they would get away with substituting pages?"

"Arrogance, money, or perhaps a little bit of both." I took a breath and then continued with, "I counted five fraudulent pages. Each of the missing authentic pages has a blackmarket value of between $20,000–$100,000, depending upon its condition and the desirability of the page."

Shaking her head, she asked, "How could you tell?"

"Are you asking how could I tell that someone panicked, or are you asking how do I know the pages are fake?"

Jessie looked perplexed by my question as she said, "The Bible pages, of course."

"The ink. Gutenberg not only developed the printing system, but he invented a new ink as well. It was varnish based, the replacement pages were printed with something else."

"How could you tell?"

"The moisture from my finger absorbed right into the print. If it was the real thing it would have remained on the surface of the letters." I took a bite of my breakfast, then added, "We'll give them enough rope to hang themselves and then we turn them in."

"To whom?"

"Capitol Police, FBI, or whoever we can find that is willing to listen." I took a few more bites of my food and then continued, "But first we need to meet John. So finish up."

Once breakfast was finished, Jessie and I walked back to the Foggy Bottom Metro station and caught the Blue Line to Arlington National Cemetery. After checking through the grave registration, we hopped on the tour bus that brought us to within walking distance of George Borne's grave.

"Now what?" asked Jessie.

"We look to see if John has left us anything."

When we got close to the Borne's headstone, Jessie said, "I see the phone, but that's all."

"Perhaps he was short on cash." I looked around and then said, "I think John's had enough time, let me call him."

With that apprehensive look of her's, Jessie said, "We really should get out of here."

I punched in John's number, and before hitting send, I said, "This should only take a moment."

"Try to keep it short."

"Don't worry, I will." When he answered, I asked, "John, did you find everything in the exact location that I told you?" I moved the phone away from my mouth, looked at Jessie and said, "John found what he needed to help us catch the bad guys. He'll be here any moment."

Before I could continue with my conversation with John, the area was inundated with black SUV's, all with flashing lights. Among the first people to step out of the lead vehicle were, Stapleton and Robert. Robert was in handcuffs.

I turned to Jessie and said, "Did I say we were meeting John Cooper? I'm sorry, I get so confused sometimes. What I meant to say was John Stapleton." Pausing for a moment, I then added, "I'm afraid he's got some bad news for you. He probably wants to tell you the same thing that he told your boyfriend, Robert."

As he cuffed her, the Federal Agent accompanying Stapleton said, "Jessica Welch, you are under arrest. You have the right to remain silent. Anything you say may be used against you in a court of law…"

Jessica looked at me and said, "How did you know?"

"I found the ink that you used, in your closet."

As Stapleton was dropping me off at the airport, he said, "Professor Doyle, I don't know how we can ever thank you."

"I'm sure you'll find a way, Mr. Librarian"

THE END

THE MYSTERY SURROUNDING AGNES

CHAPTER I

According to my best friend, Doctor John Cooper, his wife, Liz was out of town for a few days, for what apparently was none of my business. To say the least, John's loving wife has always been a bit of mystery to me. I have to say that I do like her, and it appears that she likes me as well. All and all though, there's just something about her that I just can't put my finger on. But I digress. Liz is not dining with us this evening. Tonight, it's like old times, just John and I sitting at a table at Antonio's, my favorite eatery on Federal Hill in Providence.

"Good evening gentlemen," said Antonio, "Will your lovely wife be joining us this evening, Doctor Coop?"

"Not tonight, Antonio," replied John.

Antonio poured wine into the glasses that he set before us and said, "That's a shame she's not with you Doctor Coop, but you two gentlemen enjoy your dinner anyway."

I ordered my usual; tortellini. John, on the other hand had his mind set on trying something new. Listening to him place his order, I could only imagine that his choice of this entree was not that Liz would approve of.

While finishing off the evening with a cognac, a man approached our table, looked directly at me and asked, "Professor Doyle?"

"Yes, I'm Buckley Doyle. How may I help you?"

"Professor, perhaps I'm out of line, but Antonio told me that you may be able to help me and that I should talk to you."

I looked over at Antonio. He nodded, then turned and passed through the door that led into the kitchen.

"And you would be Mr...?"

"Seagrave."

I thought to myself, "That's it, just Seagrave?" I was sure that the man standing before me was not one of those celebrities that only went by a mononymous name, so I said, "Mr. Seagrave, this is my colleague, Doctor John Cooper." I paused for a moment and continued with, "I must tell you that if you expect this conversation to continue, I suggest that you reveal your full name."

Both John and I looked up at the man and waited. With a look of anguish on his face, he said, "Seagrave. My name is Arthur Wellington Seagrave."

"Now that we have that cleared up, please have a seat."

Without saying anything, Seagrave looked at John, then over to me. Reading his body language, I said, "Mr. Seagrave, be assured that anything you say to me can be said in the presence of my colleague."

"Very well."

"Mr. Seagrave, now why don't you tell Doctor Cooper and me exactly what it is that we can help you with this evening?"

"It concerns my wife."

98

John looked at Seagrave and said, "What about her, and what is her name?"

"Her name is Agnes Seagrave and I cannot find her."

I took a sip of my cognac and then said, "Perhaps you wouldn't mind elaborating on that a bit more."

My initial analysis of Arthur Wellington Seagrave, based not only on his name, but on his attire and mannerisms as well, was that he was a man of means. Somewhat taller than John or myself, his faint accent led me to surmise that he was of English descent. He appeared to be in his mid-seventies.

Before he could begin speaking, I added, "Have you reported her missing to the police?"

"No."

"And why is that?" asked John.

"Because I have no proof that she's missing."

I looked at John, and then back at our guest and said, "Mr. Seagrave, if you have no proof that your wife is missing, then what makes you so certain that she is?"

"The urn that was returned to me after her cremation was empty."

CHAPTER II

Although chasing after empty cremation urns wasn't something that interested me, I decided to take the case as a favor to Antonio. It was apparent to me, even without asking, that the Seagrave's and Antonio had a well-established relationship. Knowing Antonio as well as I do, I had no doubt in my mind that there was a little more to the story.

John and I extended our condolences before I bid my new client a good evening. Before he left, I arranged for Seagrave to meet me at my home at 928 Benefit Street at 10:00 a.m. the next morning. I also assured John that he was excused from the meeting as I was sure that I would have the matter cleared up before Seagrave even arrived.

As John and I were about to leave, Antonio approached us and pulled out a picture of Agnes from his wallet. After listening to him talk about her, I was left with the feeling that he had a sweet spot for the late Mrs. Seagrave and was as concerned about her missing ashes as was the husband himself.

The next morning, I rose before the sun and went straight to work researching the demise of Agnes Seagrave. It appeared that dear Agnes died as a result of injuries sustained during an automobile accident. The vehicle she was driving was broadsided by a pickup truck with a drunk driver behind the steering wheel. The accident happened while she was passing through an intersection. The fifty-eight year-old woman, who was otherwise in good health, was rushed to the trauma center at Providence Hospital. Two hours later Agnes was pronounced dead.

The only other information that I could find on poor Agnes, was that she was a British national and was survived by her husband, Arthur, their daughter Kathryn and two grandchildren.

Kathryn and her children reside in Leicestershire, England where Agnes's remains were slated to be interred in a plot on the family's ancestral estate.

Digging a little deeper I discovered that the Seagrave's were actually Sir Arthur and Lady Agnes of the village that bore their last name.

Following her death, arrangements were made for her remains to be cremated and for a memorial service to be held at Regent Funeral Home in Providence. From there, the urn was to be returned to her husband for transport back to her birthplace.

I called Regent to discuss the matter. They refused to comment citing privacy concerns. I also called the morgue at the state medical examiners office. When I told them that I was Doctor John Cooper, the person on the other end informed me, off the record, that they had never received a body by that name. The call that I placed to Providence Hospital got me nowhere at all.

My next inquiry was going to involve the police, but first I wanted to talk to Arthur Seagrave. I made myself a cup of tea and waited for his arrival. Twenty minutes later I showed Seagrave into my library.

"It seems as though I owe you an apology for my lack of protocol in addressing you." I paused, and then added, "I was unaware of your title until I conducted my research."

"That's quite understandable, I assure you."

"So, would you prefer that I address you as Sir Arthur?"

"We're on the left side of the pond, Professor Doyle. You may address me as you wish. Sir Arthur, or simply Seagrave. Either is acceptable."

I smiled and said, "I'm glad that we have that settled, Sir Arthur. Please have a seat. I have a few questions."

After once again expressing my condolences for his loss, I told Sir Arthur most of what my morning's worth of research had revealed. I understood the reasoning behind his decision to have Agnes cremated here in the states before shipping her remains home to England to her final resting spot. Less red tape, but I chose not to dwell on that issue.

Instead, I asked, "At the risk of sounding, perhaps, a bit crass. When was the last time that you saw Agnes?"

"In the Emergency Room on the day of the accident."

"At Providence Hospital; correct?"

"Yes. That is correct."

I could see the pain of that day written all over his face, so I proceeded as gently as possible.

"Sir Arthur, it's important that I know the answer to my next question."

"I understand, Professor, ask what you must."

"Did you see your wife's body after she passed?"

CHAPTER III

The case of Agnes' missing ashes was becoming more complicated than I had originally thought. As much as I hated to admit it, I found myself in a bit of a quandary and thought that perhaps a little assistance from John would be helpful in order to move forward.

Much to my displeasure, the good doctor thought that his living, breathing patients were, as he put it, "More worthy of my attention than that of the missing cremated remains of Agnes Seagrave." Of course I disagreed with him, but this time to no avail.

Before my meeting with Sir Arthur concluded he told me that Agnes seemed alert by the time the ambulance crew arrived at Providence Hospital. Before he was allowed to see his wife, one of the doctors from the trauma room came out and informed him that Agnes had taken a turn for the worse. It appeared that she had suffered a severe head injury that caused a brain hemorrhage. The doctor told him that the chances of making a recovery were minimal. By the time he arrived at her bedside, Agnes was brain-dead and on a respirator.

Sir Arthur knew and understood his wife's desire for quality of life and honored it. Within forty-five minutes all signs of life had passed from Agnes's body and she was pronounced dead. That was the point at which he last saw his wife's body.

I bid Sir Arthur farewell and told him that I'd be in touch with him tomorrow.

I called John back and informed him that I needed access to his computer and that I would be at his office within the hour. On my way there, I paid Detective Frank Callahan of the Providence Police an impromptu visit.

Without getting into too much detail, I asked him to take a look at Agnes Seagrave's accident report and death certificate. My detective friend was reluctant at first. Then I reminded Callahan that he owed me a favor for solving the homicide that occurred two doors down from my place. He wasn't happy, but he told me that he'd find out what he could.

It was noon by the time I arrived at John's. The office was closed for lunch and with the exception of John, who I found sitting at his desk, the place was void of both patients and staff.

"Are you not feeling well today, Buckley?" asked John as he looked up at me from his desk. Then he added, "If you are ill, then please have a seat in the waiting room. The office reopens at 1:00 p.m., someone will see you then."

"Very funny."

"I thought so."

"I need your doctorly powers that be to access Agnes Seagrave's records on the day that she was brought into the ER at Providence Hospital."

With a frown on his face John replied, "You're serious, aren't you?"

Giving him a stone-faced look back, I said, "I've never been more serious in my life." Then with a smile I added, "Well, perhaps once or twice." With John staring at me I said, "Okay, four times at the most."

John turned to his computer and said, "Tell me what it is you're looking for."

"A copy of her ER records on the day that she was brought in following her accident."

"What else?"

"All the names of the medical professionals that were present in the trauma room and had any involvement in her treatment as well as postmortem care."

"Is that all, because most of what you're asking for is information that is confidential." Then he turned to me and added, "You've heard of HIPAA; right?"

"That, my good doctor, is exactly why you're asking and I'm not."

"Doyle, sometimes you can be a real, ass."

"As long as I'm being an ass, why don't you ask the Coroner's Office for a copy of Agnes's autopsy report and death certificate as well."

CHAPTER IV

I went back to 928 Benefit Street and waited for both Detective Callahan and John to call me with their findings. To my surprise, Callahan actually stopped by. I asked him to join me in my library where I offered him a cup of tea before inquiring about what he had found.

Either he wasn't thirsty or would have preferred coffee. Whatever his reasoning, he replied, "No thank you, Professor."

I gave the reverence of the relationship some thought and said, "Detective, I believe we know one another well enough to dispense with formalities and address each other by our Christian names." I paused for a second and then added, "You may call me Buckley."

It seemed that my comment may have caught the detective off guard and left him with a lack of words. In an effort to release him from his awkwardness, I continued with, "So Frank, it's obvious by your presence that you uncovered some information that you would like to share with me."

Callahan continued to appear a bit confused, but then said, "I have a copy of Agnes Seagrave's accident report."

"How about her death certificate?"

"That paperwork appears to be delayed at the moment." He hesitated and then added, "Before we go any further, Buckley, I need to know what this is all about."

I gave the brief exchange that had just occurred between the two of us some further thought and said, "Perhaps I was somewhat hasty with the whole first name thing."

"I agree, it didn't feel quite right."

"Detective, I was asked by the deceased's husband, Sir Arthur Seagrave, to look into why he was presented with an urn that was devoid of her remains."

"Why did he come to you and not the police?"

I hesitated for a moment, then said, "He thinks that…," I thought quickly and continued with, "perhaps her ashes were simply misplaced. Nothing criminal, so he asked me to help him find them."

"Is that why you asked me for the accident report and a copy of the death certificate?"

"Yes, that is exactly the reason."

"Apparently the coroner's office is experiencing some kind of a computer glitch, but here's the accident report."

Trying to hide my frustration, I asked, "What kind of problem would that be?"

"I couldn't tell you. I work homicide, not IT."

"Did you read the accident report, Detective?"

"As a matter of fact, I did."

"And what did it tell you?"

"That her car was hit broadside by a vehicle driven by a drunk."

I scratched my head and asked, "Anything else, Detective?"

"Yes, he was arrested for DUI."

"Do you have any information if he was later charged with death resulting?" I asked.

"It didn't say that."

"And why would that little bit of information be left out?"

Looking upset, Callahan said, "Are you trying to tell me that someone in the Police Department is conducting a cover-up?"

"I don't believe so, Detective." I paused for a moment and then added, "Somewhere else perhaps; but I believe the police to be innocent in this matter."

"And you will let me know when you think that you've figured out that detail; right."

"You'll be the first person I call, Detective."

I heard my front door open and as John walked into the library, I said to Callahan, "You have my word on it, Detective." Then I turned to John and said, "You're just in time. Detective Callahan was just leaving."

Callahan gave me the folder he had brought with him and said, "Remember Professor, keep me in the loop." Then he added, "I'll let myself out."

As he passed by John, Detective Callahan said, "Nice to see you again, Doctor."

John replied with a simple nod.

Giving Callahan enough time to vacate my home, John said, "What was that all about?"

"Missing pieces of Agnes' puzzle."

John tightened his lips for a moment and then said, "And the plot thickens."

Wasting no further time, he pulled a bunch of printouts from his bag and added, "These, my dear Buckley, may just point you in the right direction."

CHAPTER V

After reviewing the ER report line-by-line with John, I asked, "Have you ever met this Doctor…" I looked at the spelling of his name again and continued with, "S-a-z-m-e-n-i-e?"

"I have, one time, at a conference that I was presenting at."

"And?"

"And he seemed okay enough. A little young perhaps. One of those doctors who thinks he knows more than anyone else, if you know what I mean. But other than that, he seems like a regular guy."

"Well, that sounds like about every doctor I've ever met. How about Doctor Cayman?"

John shook his head and gave me, "the look". Then he replied, "I don't know Cayman, or anything about him for that matter."

I watched as a frown grew on John's face as he read the ER report a little further. A few seconds later he said, "Give me your laptop, will you?" He typed in a few search words and asked, "Do you know your blood type?"

"AB, why?"

"Around ninety-nine point two percent of the world's population fall into the major blood groups such as A, B, AB, and O. Some being positive and some being negative. That's where you and I fall, and that's good."

"Your point?"

John turned my laptop so that the screen was facing me and said, "That leaves zero point eight percent who do not fall into the most common groups." He gave me a minute to look at the information on the screen, and then added, "Unfortunate those individuals have extremely rare blood types like Oh, CDE or CwD, as you can see here."

"And Agnes Seagrave had one of those?"

John shook his head and answered, "No."

"Then what is your point?"

John scrolled a little further down the screen and said, "According to the lab report, Agnes bears the rarest of all, Bombay Blood Type hh." Then he added, "I've heard about this, but in all my years of practice I have never come across an actual patient with this rear type of blood."

"Just how rare is it?"

"It's extremely rear. Less than ten people in the world are documented to have Bombay Blood Type hh."

"Well, that's certainly sends up a red flag."

John turned my laptop back his way and as he entered more search words he said, "Sadly, there is no information in the international registry of any available donors with Bombay Blood Type hh."

"What do people like Agnes do when they need blood?"

"Besides hoping for a miracle, there's basically nothing they can do."

"And so it would be the same for others like her as well."

"You're exactly right."

I got on the phone and called Seagrave. Trying not to set off any alarm bells, I asked, "By any chance do you know what your wife's blood type was?"

"I know that it was very special, but I have no idea of the exact letters involved." There was a moment of silence before he added, "We were married for thirty-five years and in all that time she'd never really been sick a day in her life." There was another pause and then he said, "Why do you ask?"

I replied, "It's just one of the miscellaneous items that I was looking into."

He seemed satisfied with that explanation, however I now worried about his daughter and grandchildren well being.

When I finished my phone conversation with Sir Arthur, I turned to John and asked, "How did you make out with the Coroner's report?"

"I couldn't find anything. It's like she was never there."

"Perhaps it's time that we pay the coroner a little visit."

CHAPTER VI

Rhode Island has one central coroner's office and it's about a five-minute drive from 928 Benefit Street. As usual, John drove. When we arrived, the two of us went inside, signed the visitor's log and then took the elevator one floor down to the morgue.

Fortunately for us, the assistant coroner on duty was a doctor friend of John's who was moonlighting on the evening shift. As a favor to John, he let us in.

"For what am I bestowed the honor, John?"

"James, this is a colleague of mine, Buckley Doyle." Under the circumstances I nodded and forwent my usual handshake. Then John added, "We would like to take a look at the autopsy report for one Agnes Seagrave."

He swung his computer in front of him and entered her name. With his eyes still on his monitor he said, "You did say Agnes, right?"

I replied, "Yes, Agnes Seagrave." Then I spelled her name out for him.

"Are you sure she died in Rhode Island?"

"Yes, Agnes died at Providence Hospital a week and a half ago. Her death was a result of an automobile accident."

James looked up and said, "Are you sure about that?"

"According to the ER report she did," replied John.

"You might want to try the holding morgue at the hospital."

"Do you have the name of a contact person over there?" I asked in the hope of gaining easy access.

"As a matter of fact I do. A Doctor Sazmenie runs that department." Then James added, "I'm sorry I couldn't have been more of a help."

John and I looked at each other at the same time, and then I turned to James and said, "Thank you, Doctor. You've been more helpful than you can imagine."

On our way back to his car John said, "What do you think the odds of that are?"

"About the same as Agnes' blood type." Then I added, "We need to dig a little deeper into Sazmenie's situation. And we need to get into that morgue, tonight."

As we got into the car, John replied, "That shouldn't be too hard. After all, I am a doctor with hospital privileges, one being Providence Hospital."

Fifteen minutes later we were across town and headed down to the tunnel system that lay beneath Providence Hospital. Along with the facility's laundry and maintenance areas, it's where the morgue is located.

Before we descended down the dark stairwell, I followed John into the doctor's lounge where he grabbed a couple of white lab coats. John had his hospital badge with him and attached it over his pocket. I, on the other hand, had a doctor's coat with Providence Hospital embroidered on the front. I let John lead the way and in no time we were standing at the keypad that secured the entrance to the morgue. The swipe of John's card was followed by the click of the lock. With a push of the door switch, we were inside the morgue.

Right off the bat I could tell that we were alone. All the lights were off and it was spooky. A second later John found the switch and the place was illuminated. Apparently it was a slow night, there were no bodies lying on slabs.

John went right over to the refrigerated drawers and started reading the labels. Following his lead I did the same. A quick scan revealed no Agnes Seagrave.

"Look for the Jane Does," said John.

Remembering what Agnes looked like from the picture that Antonio had shown us, we opened the first drawer labeled Jane Doe.

After sliding the tray out, I turned to John and said, "Definitely not her."

John opened the second door and, like that of the first, the corpse inside was not Agnes Seagrave.

We started over. John began searching every draw from the left and I went from the right. On his third draw, John said, "I can't say for sure, but based what I'm looking at, I'm pretty sure I found Agnes."

John was still staring down at Agnes when I approached the extracted draw. After a quick look, I said, "I think we need to call Detective Callahan."

CHAPTER VII

The phone rang seven times before the voice on the other end answered, "Homicide, Callahan."

"Detective, we've found Agnes Seagrave's body."

"You mean her ashes?"

"No, we found her body." Then I added, "And I think you need to get over here as quickly as possible."

There was a pause, and then Callahan asked, "Where are you?"

"I'm at the morgue at Providence Hospital." Without saying another word, I hung up.

Twenty minutes later Callahan joined John and me in the hospital morgue. John reopened the draw and withdrew the tray.

Callahan looked back at me and said, "Where the hell's her face?"

As John pushed the drawer closed he replied, "Most likely with the rest of her other vital organs." He paused for a moment then added, "Of course, the only way we can tell for sure that this is indeed Agnes Seagrave, is to conduct another autopsy."

Not looking at Callahan, I said, "I'm sure you'll find that her blood was removed as well."

Looking puzzled, Callahan said, "What do you mean, her blood?"

117

I replied, "As it turns out, Agnes had an extremely rare blood type, which makes it, as well as most of her body parts extremely valuable."

"Who the hell would do something like this to another human being?"

John raised his eyebrows and said, "Follow the money, Detective."

Adding to John's advice I said, "I'd suggest that you begin your search with Doctor Sazmenie. He's young and presumably in a lot of debt. He was present in the ER when Agnes was brought in, and as it turns out, this Doctor is also in charge of the very morgue in which we are now standing."

Callahan pulled out his notepad and said, "How do you spell this guy's name?"

Within an hour of Detective Callahan's arrival, the morgue in the basement of Providence Hospital was considered a crime scene. After the body, which we were quite certain was Agnes' was removed from the area and brought to the Coroner's Office, John and I accompanied Callahan back to police headquarters.

Once there, Callahan wasted no time in issuing an APB for Doctor Sazmenie. He also ordered a forensic audit on the doctor's financial well being.

"Why don't you two come with me," said Callahan.

As we walked into a conference room, Callahan introduced us to his boss, Captain Russell and his associate Detective Paul-Blanc, whom I had met previously.

118

Then he turned to me and said, "Please tell us your theory regarding the demise of Agnes Seagrave."

After explaining Sir Arthur's request for help finding his wife's ashes, I went into what I discovered along the way by saying, "According to the first responders report, Agnes' head wound was superficial at best, and she was alert and active upon her arrived at the ER. The initial emergency room notes also confirmed this. In fact, it wasn't until after the trauma team was dismissed and Agnes's lab results were confirmed by Doctor Sazmenie, that she took a turn for the worse."

"Why don't you tell the captain exactly what those lab results revealed about Mrs. Seagrave," requested Callahan.

I gave it a moment and then said, "Agnes Seagrave possessed the rarest of all blood types, Bombay Blood Type hh, worth approximately ten thousand dollars a pint on the black market. Given that the average person has about eleven pints, that's equivalent to roughly one hundred and ten thousand dollars." After viewing a few raised eyebrows, I added, "In order for the blood to retain that value, it had to be removed from her body while she was still alive."

After absorbing what I had just told them, the captain said, "So you're telling us that Agnes Seagrave was murdered for her blood?"

"That and her organs as well. Because of her blood type, things like her heart, lungs, liver, kidneys, eyes, oh... and let's not forget her tissues, would fetch a handsome price on the black market."

Callahan looked at his Captain and said, "Her face was also removed."

The Captain wrinkled his nose and said, "What else was removed from this poor lady?"

"We'll have to wait for a full autopsy report to determine that."

CHAPTER VIII

After providing Callahan and his boss with a potential motive for Agnes Seagrave's demise, John and I returned to 928 Benefit Street and discussed the daunting task of informing Sir Arthur of our findings.

Under the circumstances, I thought it best if both John and I went to him. I called and made arrangements to meet him at his home in East Greenwich, a small bayside community in the southern part of the state. It was 9:00 p.m. when we arrived at his door. No one wants to give or receive news of this type at any time, much less at this late hour. But I thought that it was best that he hear it from me and not through breaking news on television.

I could tell by the look on his face when he answered the door that he knew exactly why we were there. Sir Arthur led us into his living room. He took the news as well as could be expected.

After making sure that Sir Arthur was okay enough to be left alone, John and I departed. It was ten thirty in the evening when John dropped me off at my place and then drove to his own empty home.

The next morning brought a degree of normalcy to our lives. John was back at his office seeing patients and I was presenting a lecture on pre-twentieth century literature to my favorite students, the ones with mush filled skulls.

My lecture was interrupted by Detective Callahan walking in and letting the door slam behind him.

I gave my students an assignment to write an essay, on the relevance of Pen Names and the meaning behind them during the eighteenth century, then proceeded to collect my belongings.

While I was packing up, Callahan approached the podium and said, "Professor Doyle, do you have a moment?"

I was expecting good news, but my expectations were shattered when Callahan said, "We found Doctor Sazmenie. He was in the draw adjacent to Mrs. Seagrave."

"I wasn't expecting that," I replied.

"Me either." Then he added, "The forensic audit we ran on him came back clean as well."

"How about Agnes's autopsy results?"

"You were spot on with that one."

I took a deep breath that was filled with disappointment and asked, "What now, Detective?"

"We've arrested Doctor Cayman at Logan Airport in Boston. He was about to board a plane to Lisbon. He had a one-way ticket and three hundred and fifty-thousand dollars in cash tucked away in a carryon. I thought you'd like to know."

"Did you get a confession out of him?"

"Not yet, but he's being extradited back to Rhode Island where we'll charge him with the murders of Agnes Seagrave and Omar Sazmenie as well as the illegal trafficking of human body parts. We also arrested the owner of Regent Funeral Home and charged him with accessory to the fact."

I thanked Callahan and then called John.

That evening I paid a visit to Antonio's. I wasn't hungry, but I asked for a table anyway. When Antonio saw me, he came over and said, "Mister Buck, it is so nice to see you this evening." Then with a big smile he asked, "Where is Doctor Coop and his lovely wife Lizzy? Don't tell me you eating alone tonight?"

"I'm afraid so, Antonio." I took a deep breath and then added, "Antonio, sit down for a minute. There's something I need to tell you."

"What is it Mister Buck? You seem so sad tonight."

Later I walked back to 928 Benefit Street. When I got there I sat down in my library, poured myself a glass of cognac and proceeded to get drunk.

THE END

THE HOWL
IN
THE NIGHT

CAPTER I

I closed the book I'd been reading for the past couple of evenings. It was a gift from Mrs. Jones next door. Every time our paths would cross, she'd ask if I read it yet and to let her know how I liked the ending. She's a nice enough old lady, so I'd always tell her that I'll get to it soon. I felt obligated to read it, but even after my second cognac and as many attempts, I'm finding it boring.

It was late, but I poured myself a third glass of my favorite libation, took a sip and stepped out onto the deck outside my library doors. I pulled a couple of chairs together, sat in one, put my feet up on the other and looked out at the city lights. I don't know how long I was out there before the silence was broken by the sound of the howl in the night. I found it rather annoying.

I punched some numbers into my phone, and when John answered, I said, "Can you hear that?" Then I held the phone out at arms length.

When I put the phone back to my ear and was about to speak, all I could hear John say was, "Do you have any idea what time it is?"

"Of course I do, it's 3:00 a.m." Before I had a chance to say anything more, the phone went dead. I thought it rather rude of the person that I considered to be my best friend to hang up on me.

127

THE HOWL IN THE NIGHT

Left with no one to complain to, I sipped my drink and continued listening to the howling hound. When I couldn't stand it anymore, I got up and went to bed until the sun was starting it's day.

Later that morning I went back out onto my deck. It was a Saturday so the hustle and bustle of the weekday was partially diminished. I could still detect what I was sure was the same annoying dog. Going back inside, I made myself a light breakfast, brewed a cup of tea and carried my plate and cup outside onto my deck. The hound was still howling.

I called John again. When he answered he said, "Do you have any idea what time it is?"

"Yes, it's six o'clock, time to get up." Again the phone went dead.

I called him back. This time when he answered he said, "What is it, Doyle?"

I could tell that he was mad by the fact that he addressed me by my surname. I chose to ignore that and said, "You need to come over here right now."

"Mister Annoying, why is it that I need to do that, especially at this time of day?"

"I'm afraid that there is something very sinister occurring somewhere in the vicinity of 928 Benefit Street."

There was a hesitation on John's part, but when he spoke, he said, "What makes you so certain that there is something so terribly wrong over there, other than you, of course?"

"The howl in the night. That's what."

CHAPTER II

An hour later, John walked into my library where I was just finishing my third serving of English Breakfast Tea. While saluting him with my cup, I said, "What took you so long."

"The only reason I came to 928 was in the hope that you'd stop calling me." Then he added, "This was the first Saturday morning that Liz and I have had together in weeks. And I don't mind telling you that she's as upset as I am."

"Oh good, she's back. I was beginning to get worried."

"Don't change the subject."

"And don't bother sitting down. I called you for a reason."

John shook his head and replied, "I can just imagine."

I pointed to the door and said, "We're going for a walk."

"And why are we doing that?"

"To locate the hound. Didn't you listen to any part of my phone calls."

"Which reminds me, your calls were annoying. Furthermore, I don't like receiving prank calls from you or anyone else. Especially when they come in the middle of the night. Must I remind you yet again, that there are laws against that?"

I grinned and said, "Spin it as you like, but lets get started, shall we."

As soon as we stepped outside I could hear it. Faint, but still audible and coming from somewhere off to my left.

Cupping my hands to my ears, I said, "Hear it?"

"No, I do not."

By this time the baying had stopped, but I didn't tell John. We just kept walking in the direction from where I last heard the sound coming. Before long we found ourselves approaching the northern section of Benefit Street.

"Shall we head back to your place, Buckley?" Before I could answer, he added, "I'm being honest with you, Doyle, I haven't heard anything that even slightly resembles a barking or howling dog."

Realizing that John was beginning to become irritated with the situation, or maybe even with me, I said, "Perhaps it was nothing."

John didn't comment. I looked around, and then we headed back. When we arrived at my front door, John bid me a good day, got into his car and drove off. I, on the other hand, retraced my footsteps. I knew deep in my gut that these sounds existed and that there was a reason behind them.

Unlike my quiet journey with John just moments ago, this time I was guided along my way toward the distant baying. About a block away I was following the canine sounds which lead me up the hill to Congdon Street. With every step I took, the hound's bay became more pronounced. I followed it along until I reached Prospect Terrace Park where the proud statue of Roger

Williams resides. It was here that the bay of a hound turned to that of a whimpering pet. I watched as the poor dog sat up, became silent and fixed his eyes on me.

As if to say, "Help" he stood up and disappeared around to the front of the monument. Before I managed to climb over the wrought iron rails that encircle the statue, the dog stuck his head back around the corner. With my footing back on the granite base surrounding the monument, he once more disappeared from my sight.

I found him at the foot of the statue of Roger Williams. He was lying on the cold stone huddled against the body of a disheveled man.

"It's okay, boy," Were the only words I said to the dog as I checked his companion for any signs of life. Seconds later I called 911.

I reached down to pet the poor hound. In response, the dog rested his chin on the lap of the man whom I could only assume had been his best friend.

Minutes later the area was abuzz with first responders.

THE HOWL IN THE NIGHT

CHAPTER III

The hound had a rope tied to his collar. He never moved as I bent down and picked up his homemade leash. I looked down at him and watched his eyes follow every movement of the EMT's as they worked on the lifeless body of his owner.

"Nice dog, yours?"

I recognized the voice, it was Detective Callahan. I turned my head his way and replied, "No. From what I can tell, that's his master over there."

"Homeless man, homeless dog."

"Do you know who he was, Detective?"

"Not yet, but it doesn't look like there was any foul play involved." Then he looked down at the dog and added, "I'll call animal control and have him picked up."

I waited around until they arrived. It was obvious by the way the poor hound was acting that he knew he'd never see his master again. Oddly enough though, when the dog officer told him to get in, he looked around one last time and hopped right into the back of the truck.

When the officer was done, I turned to him and said, "Seems like a nice enough dog, probably make a good pet for some family."

"Nobody would want a dog like that." As he walked to the front of his truck he added, "I'm afraid he'll just be put down."

133

Minutes after Animal Control drove off, the Coroner's vehicle did the same. I hung around for a while contemplating the sadness of the hound and that of his master. I then walked back home and took a nap on the couch.

Later that afternoon John called and asked what time I wanted to meet Liz and him for dinner at Antonio's. I made up some cockamamie excuse about needing to prepare my Monday afternoon lecture. But truth have it, I just couldn't get the morning's events out of my mind. I poured myself a cognac, sat down on a chair on my deck and listened for the hound.

It was Monday morning when Detective Callahan called me and said. "The guy you found Saturday, he was homeless. Based on what little information we've managed to collect, he was a Vet named, William Perry, forty-five, no known address or next of kin."

"What was the cause of death?"

"Natural causes. I thought you'd like to know."

After I hung up with Callahan, I contacted Annie, my most reliable grad student and made arrangements for her to cover my afternoon lecture. With that matter taken care of, I found my way across town to the Coroner's office.

After introducing myself to the clerk, I said, "I'm here regarding William Perry."

In a polite tone she replied, "Your name and relationship to the deceased?"

"Buckley Doyle, I'm a friend."

"Someone will be with you in a minute, Mr. Doyle."

A minute turned into twenty. When I was ready to get up and ask if they had forgotten me, I heard a voice say, "Professor Doyle, nice to see you again." I looked around to see John's moonlighting doctor friend, James. Then he added, "What brings you to the morgue on such a lovely Monday morning?"

"I'm looking to gather some information on one of your clients."

"The homeless fellow?"

"Actually his name is William Perry. He's a veteran, with no known next of kin. I just want to make sure he gets the proper military funeral due him."

James replied, "I understand, Professor. We've already contacted Veteran Affairs. They claim that they have no record of him ever serving in the armed forces."

"Can you give me a name over there?"

"The man you want to speak to is Lawrence Goodwin." Then James added, "He's the administrator."

CHAPER IV

"Do you have any idea how many 'William Perry's' served in the Army alone?" Then Goodwin added, "Without more information to go by, I'm afraid there's nothing I can do."

"So we just throw his body to the wolves and say the hell with it?"

"Get me his service number, date of service, unit, anything like that and I'll see what I can do."

I left Lawrence Goodwin's office with just what I went in with, nothing. All I had to work with was a name and picture that James had taken of him laying there on the autopsy table.

On my way home, I stopped at the city pound to see if Perry's hound had a new home yet. The place was appalling. When we got to his cage, the homeless hound sat up and looked at me as if he had just seen an old friend. The volunteer who lead me out back to the kennel said, "I guess this is the one you're looking for."

"No takers yet?"

"I'm afraid the only way out of here for this guy is through the cremation furnace." Then she added, "Too bad, he's a nice dog."

An hour later I was sitting in my library and the hound, who I named Fella for lack of anything better, was sitting in the hallway staring at me. I poured myself a cognac, and Fella sat there and watched me drink it. It was a quiet moment.

Finally I gave in and said, "Are you hungry, Fella?"

He just sat there and looked at my eyes. I opened a can of hash, spooned it into a bowl and set it down in front of him. He sniffed it, looked back up at me, but wanted nothing to do with it. I placed a bowl of water next to the food and got the same reaction. I called John.

When he answered, I said, "I've got a problem."

"What is it this time?"

"I think there's something wrong with Fella."

After a short pause, John replied, "Fella, who?"

"The hound."

"The what?"

"The dog."

"When the hell did you get a dog? Better still, why on earth would you ever get a dog?"

"It's a long story."

"With you, it always is."

In short, John told me that when Fella gets hungry, he'll eat, and when he gets thirsty, he'll drink. John also told me that I should do everything within my power to take him back to wherever he came from.

Throughout my whole conversation with John, Fella just sat there and continued to stare at me. I tried staring him down, but he won every time. I thought perhaps a walk was in order. I grabbed my hat and coat then tied the rope to the collar that Fella came with. Then Fella and I headed toward downtown.

Fella, as it turned out, was a great walker. No leading, tugging or lagging behind, he just walked along beside me like we'd been doing this for years.

By chance, Fella and I ended up along the Providence River and made our way to the area of the World War II Memorial. There weren't a lot of people walking around down there. One man however, caught my attention. Every time I looked around, he seemed to be watching us.

I took the initiative and said, "May I help you?"

He looked at me kind of funny and asked, "Where did you get that dog, Mister?"

CHAPTER V

I tugged on his rope and said, "Come on, Fella."

Staring at us, the man said, "His name's not Fella, it's Reggie."

"You know this dog?"

"You steal this dog?"

"No, did you know his owner?"

The man turned and walked quickly towards the stand of trees that bordered the monument.

I shouted, "Wait." When he didn't stop, I added, "I need to ask you about William Perry."

Fella and I followed him, but he seemed to disappear by the time we made our way to the other side of the trees. I looked down at Fella and said, "If he knows who you are, boy, then he's the man we need to talk to." All I got in return from Fella was a stare. So I said, "Let's go home…" I paused before I finished what I was saying, gave it a little thought, then finished my sentence with, "Reggie." I think I may have noticed a slight wag of his tail.

When we got back to 928 Benefit Street, Reggie stopped in his usual spot outside my library doorway. He sat there and watched as I poured myself a drink. Just as I was about to sit down in my favorite chair, there was pounding on my front door. Without making a sound, Reggie turned his head and looked in that direction. Following me to the door, Reggie stayed by my side and waited for me to open it.

When I opened the door the man facing me said, "I came to visit Reggie."

He was the homeless man who knew Reggie's name. I looked at him for a few seconds and said, "Please come in, I'm sure he'll enjoy having company."

I walked back to my library, gestured to him to have a seat and said, "Would you care for a drink?"

"No. I've been clean for two years."

I looked at my glass sitting on the end table and said, "Perhaps something to eat then?"

"I'm not here for a handout mister, I just need to know why you have Reggie, that's all."

"Did you know William Perry?"

"Yeah, I know Wild Bill. What about him?"

"He's dead, and that's why I now have his dog."

Our visitor sat there for a while and then said, "What happened to him?"

"He just died. I found his lifeless body Saturday on Congdon Street."

"Guess that's why I haven't seen him around."

"I was told he was a Vet. Do you know anything about that?"

After looking off in the distance, our visitor said, "Yeah, had lots of medals and things. Kept 'em wrapped up with all his stuff. He'd like to take 'em out and tell everyone how he got 'em."

"Do you know where William, I mean, Wild Bill, kept his things?"

"He used to move 'em around a lot, but I know he tucked some things up under one of the Water Fire bridges." A few seconds later he said, "Why you so interested in Wild Bill anyway?"

"I want to make sure that he receives a proper funeral, that's all."

"The type with the flags and guns?"

I shook my head and said, "Yes. A full military funeral at the Veterans' Cemetery, complete with a bugler, an honor guard and all the respect that is due a Veteran."

With a hint of a smile, he said, "Wild Bill would like that. He'd like that a lot."

CHAPTER VI

Even after having company, Reggie still wouldn't eat or move from his special spot. One good thing though, he did drink some water. It was after midnight when I tied Reggie's rope to his collar and said, "Come on boy, we're going for another walk."

For the second time in as many hours, Reggie and I were walking along the Providence River. This time, however, we were headed in the opposite direction towards the bridges that span the canal and walkways down by Water Place Park. Some place down here were William Perry's belongings, or so I was led to believe.

To say that this place wasn't spooky at this time of night was like saying that the homeless people down here had a place to go. It was and they didn't. Reggie and I had already checked the underside of the first bridge and were on our way to the next one. I thought of calling John and telling him to meet me. I checked the time on my phone. It was 1:00 a.m. He never likes it when I call this late, so Reggie and I continued along without his help.

The second bridge was narrower than the first. It also was constructed with an open metal framework. Stuffed up amongst the steel supports, I could see what looked like a bundle of something. I looked down at Reggie and said, "What do you think that is, boy?" His reply was in the form of staring up at what I was looking at. I shined the flashlight app of my phone on it and added, "Looks like we may have found it, boy."

142

I climbed up on the railing, grabbed the structure above and made my way to a point over the water where I could reach for what I was after. When I got back on solid ground I unwrapped the bundle and looked through it. Everything that lay before me obviously belonged to a woman. Reggie looked at me like I had just committed a crime, and to be honest that's how I felt. I carefully wrapped everything back up the way I found it and placed it back to where I found it. On my way back to solid ground I heard a splash. It wasn't until I was back on the walkway with Reggie that I realized that the splashing sound was my cell phone hitting the water.

Despite the fact that the one device that contained my calendar, contact list and photos had found a new home at the bottom of the river, we made our way to the third, and final, bridge only to find a man sleeping under it on a piece of cardboard. Both Reggie and I stepped over him. He didn't budge an inch and I wondered if he was even alive.

This end of the walkway was the darkest area that we traveled through and under the bridge was even darker. Without my phone I had no flashlight. Reggie and I turned around and headed back. An hour later we were at the front door of 928 Benefit Street.

Once inside, I again scooped out some fresh hash in hopes that Reggie would eat. Of course he just sat in his spot in the doorway and stared at me. Exhausted I sat in my favorite chair and fell in to a deep sleep.

With a stiff neck and a headache I awoke to sunlight shining in on me through the deck door as if telling me, "Wake up Buckley, time to rise and shine."

When I was somewhat coherent, I realized that Reggie wasn't in his spot staring at me as he'd been doing since he became my roommate. Instead, I found him laying on the floor next to the front door. He looked up at me, then returned his focus of attention back to the door.

"What is it boy, need to go out?"

Not expecting any kind of reply, I tied his rope to his collar and unlocked the door. Without any command Reggie moved out of the way as I pulled it open. Our path was blocked by a bundle wrapped in an old wool blanket. For the first time since I picked Reggie up at the pound, he actually wagged his tail.

"What is it, Boy?"

I looked up and down the street, but saw no one. I picked up the bundle and closed the door. Before I returned to my library, I peered through the sidelight and watched as last nights visitor stepped from the bushes and walked south along Benefit Street.

I looked down at Reggie and said, "Come on boy, I think this is for you."

CHAPTER VII

To say that the bundle that was left at my front door was a bit aromatic was an understatement I carried it into my Library anyway and set it down on the couch. Reggie followed me all the way in and hopped right up there with it and begin to sniff and lick the blanket. I knew right then that this was Wild Bill's stuff.

I untied the cord that was holding the bundle together and unrolled it. Deep in the middle was a dented coffee can. Inside the can, I found William Perry's service medals. I looked at each one and placed them in a neat row on the coffee table. There were eight in all; two campaign metals, one for Afghanistan and one for Iraq. The others were three Purple Hearts, two Bronze Stars and a Silver Star.

I looked at Reggie and said, "Looks like your Wild Bill was quite the soldier."

The inside of the coffee can was lined with papers. I pulled them out, unfolded them and read what was printed on them. The first one was his Honorable Discharge.

The rest of the morning was spent in Lawrence Goodwin's office at Veterans Affairs.

That evening I met John and Liz at Antonio's on the Hill for dinner and drinks. I drank more than I ate. John still thought that I was nuts for taking in the dog, but when I showed them Reggie's picture on my new phone, Liz's heart melted.

As she gave me my phone back, she said, "A dog will be good for you, Buckley."

"Until I can find him a good home at least."

Liz rolled her eyes and smiled.

When we were ready to leave, Antonio handed me a take-out container and said, "Take this home with you, Mister Buck. You might be hungry later."

I thanked Antonio, and before we left the table I asked John and Liz if they'd mind accompanying me to Wild Bill's funeral two days later. Without hesitation they both agreed.

When I got back to 928 Benefit Street, I scraped my tortellini into Reggie's bowl, tapped my foot on the floor next to it and told him to eat. I only said it once before he started to gobble it up. Leftovers, I should have known. After he ate, Reggie and I took a walk down to the riverfront.

Two days later John, Liz, myself, the homeless man who preferred to remain nameless, and Reggie stood beside Wild Bill's flag-draped casket.

Liz was the only one of us who flinched when the three volleys were fired in rapid succession. Reggie stood there as if at attention until the bugler played taps at which time he lowered his head in apparent sadness.

When the Honor Guard finished folding the American flag and presenting it to me, I placed it on the empty chair next to Reggie.

When the ceremony concluded I invited everyone to join me at Antonio's for a bite to eat. When we ordered, the homeless man asked for his in a take-out container and so did I.

Later at home I scraped my tortellini into Reggie's bowl. When he was done eating, he walked into his library, hopped up on his couch and fell asleep. As it turns out, Reggie snores.

THE END

WINTERS

DEATH ROOM

CHAPTER I

Once again, I found myself seated at my usual table at Antonio's enjoying an evening of fine dining with the Cooper's. Being creatures of habit, Liz and I had ordered our same old favorites. She, shrimp Diavolo over linguine, and for myself, a plate of tortellini in a garlic and butter sauce. Always the adventurous one, John had set himself up and was now forced to anguish over the chef's special, Rigatoni con la pajata . It didn't look appealing to me, and although John kept saying that it was delicious, I could tell by the look on his face every time he took a bite of his culinary delight, that it was as disgusting as it appeared on his plate. I wondered if John even knew that what he was eating consisted of not only rigatoni, but stuffed veal bowels. I'd categorize this as an Italian version of haggis, both disgusting.

About half way through our dinner my attention was drawn to the presence of a man I was not accustomed to seeing in Antonio's. At first the stranger seemed to spend a considerable amount of time with the hostess. My supposition as to his purpose for choosing this eatery was heightened when instead of being seated, he was directed to Antonio himself. From my vantage point, their discussion did not appear to be confrontational, but one one of a serious nature directed.

I had to force myself to ignore sight of their exchange and instead re-engaged in conversation with my dinner companions. Toward the end of my meal I once again spotted this man who was now seated solo and appeared to be truly enjoying the Chef's special. I gave the matter no further thought and returned my attention once more to John and Liz.

I was about to opt for an espresso instead of my usual after dinner glass of cognac when this unknown man stepped up to our table and said, "Professor Doyle?"

Looking up, I rendered my usual reply, "Yes. I'm Buckley Doyle. How may I help you?"

"Is there some place where we can speak in private?"

"I assure you that whatever you have to say to me, can be said in front of my two colleagues."

A concerned look fell over the man's face that left me with the impression that this stranger was contemplating turning around and walking away. I gave my unwelcome guest a few moments to determine his fate and said, "Perhaps you'll be a bit more at ease if you were to tell me your name."

"I'd rather not at this point."

With a look on my face that reflected a slight annoyance, I clarified his apparent apprehension with, "Then I'm afraid our business here has come to an end and therefore, I must bid you a good evening."

In return, the man replied, "Thank you for your time, Professor Doyle." He then turned and solemnly walked away.

John leaned into the table and in a soft voice said, "Strange fellow; wouldn't you say?"

Liz added, "I wonder what he wanted?"

I could see in my periphery that the man turned and started to walk back toward our table. I sparked the Cooper's curiosity by saying, "I think we're about to find out."

Once again standing before me, our intruder stood silent for a moment. Looking directly at me, he said, "My name is Doctor Steven Winters, and I need you to help me with a murder."

I leaned slightly back in my chair and said, "I'm sorry, Doctor Winters, but I'm fresh out of murder. That being said, the best advice I can give you is to contact your local police department." I paused, gave the man a brief smile and then added, "Again sir, I bid you a good evening."

After the man walked away from the table for the second time, John shook his head and said, "I've got to hand it to you Buck, you do have a knack for attracting the weird ones."

"I take it then that our Doctor Winters is not in your medical circle of friends."

John shook his head and replied, "Never saw or heard of him until right now."

Liz didn't add to her husband's comment; instead choosing to grab my hand in hers and squeezed it gently.

I gave Liz's hand a squeeze of my own and replied, "Perhaps it's time to call it an evening."

Ten minutes after the Coopers dropped me off at 928 Benefit Street, the knocker on the front door could be heard throughout my entire home.

Expecting to see either John or Liz standing there, I opened the door and before looking up, asked, "Forget something?"

Shifting my focus of attention from the door lock, to the person I was addressing, I found Doctor Winters standing there and staring straight into my eyes.

Taken aback and apprehensive of his presence at my threshold, I said, "Doctor Winters, are you by any chance stalking me?"

With a confused look on his face, Winters replied, "Certainly not, Professor Doyle." Winters appeared as though he was contemplating his next words before he asked, "May I come in?"

"Repeating your words of a moment ago, Doctor, certainly not." Giving the situation a bit more thought, I added, "Sir, for the third and hopefully final time, I bid you a good evening."

"I implore you to listen to what I have to say, Professor."

I closed my eyes for a moment in disbelief of what I was about to say. When I opened them, I replied, "Thirty-seconds, Doctor Winters. That's the amount of time I'll allow you to state your case."

"Thank you, Professor."

"And now you have twenty-eight seconds."

"As I briefly mentioned to you earlier at the restaurant, I need your help with a murder..."

I interrupted Winters' attempt to explain and said, "This is the second time that you asked if I would help you with a murder." Pausing for a moment, I continued with, "I'm not sure why you're under the belief that I'm in the murder business, but let me assure you, sir, that I am not."

"Professor Doyle, if I mislead you or offended you in any way, I'm sincerely sorry. What I'm trying to say is that I need you to help me solve murder case, or what I believe to be one."

"I don't mean to disappoint you, Doctor Winters, but my detective days are behind me now. So, once again I suggest that you take your concerns to the police." I pursed my lips and added, "And with that advice, your allotted time has expired and I bid you farewell, sir."

Showing the Doctor Winters to the door, I waited in the open doorway to make sure my late night visitor truly left my property.

The evening had cooled off substantially since John and Liz had dropped me off at my front door. The chill of the air was comforting and the fact that my unwanted house guest was gone made me more relaxed. I remained in the open doorway and watched as my stalker walked to his car, got in and drive off in the direction of downtown. When I felt assured that my annoying visitor was indeed gone for the evening, I closed the door and turned off the front light.

Before leaving the foyer, I took a moment to digest the evening's events. Still in disbelief of the doctor's persistence, my thought process was interrupted by the now annoying sound of the door knocker once again as it struck in rapid succession.

Angry, I opened the door prepared with a threat for my visitor, that if he didn't stop harassing me, I would summon the police.

My hastily contrived warning was circumvented by the fact that Doctor Winters had been replaced by another visitor of the night. Unfortunately for me, the doctor's replacement was standing on my top stair with a gun in his hand; it was pointed directly at me.

In the words of his predecessor, he uttered, "May I come in, Professor Doyle?"

Before I had a chance to respond to the would-be invader's request, the gun wielding man raised his arm and pistol-whipped me. As I fell to the floor, my head pounding and vision blurred, I could barely see the intruder's arm as it came at me again. This time things went dark…

CHAPTER II

I slowly awoke, not fully coherent and with a pounding headache. The stench of decaying flesh wafted by me. Disoriented, I placed both hands around my head in an attempt to ease the pain. Opening my eyes, I found only total darkness before me. Realizing that the problem was not with my vision, but a result of my environment, I released my hands from my head hold, held them in front of my eyes and stared at them to no avail.

"Why does my hand feel wet?" I asked myself in a voice just over an audible tone. "Why is everything so dark?" I rubbed my eyes and pushed myself up with my elbows. I tried to look around and was still unable to see anything before me. My thought process added, "Where the hell am I?"

I soon realized that I was in some kind of room, but didn't know where or why I was here. Wherever this place was, it was totally dark and accompanied by the unforgettable stench of death. More concerns began to fill my head. It was apparent that there was no one else in this room to answer any of my questions.

Now on my hands and knees, I made my way to the edge of the room and thankfully felt a wall. Using the surface as an aid, I made it to my feet. The darkness that encircled me left me disoriented and a little wobbly now that I was standing. Placing my hand in front of my face, I could feel my breath on my palm, but as before I still could not make out so much as an outline of even a single digit of my hand.

My situation immediately brought back memories of a similar experience from my past. While on patrol as a member of the military, our team was caught in a horrendous storm while traversing the side of a mountain. We were deep within a hostile area in a foreign country. On this moonless night I found myself separated from the others and ended up huddled against a tree to prevent myself from being washed back down the mountainside. Similar to back then I was only able to find objects by touch. Unlike my current situation, my vision was temporarily restored with each of the endless lightning strikes that were happening all around me. Morning could not come soon enough back then.

All I knew right now was that I was trapped somewhere that was just as dark and just as hostile as that mountainside. The difference this time was that I wasn't sure morning would ever come. Unlike then, I had no clue as to what time it was, nor did I know how long I was unconscious.

Using the wall as a guided, I shuffled along the edge hoping to find any sign of a way out. A half-dozen paces from where I had made it to my feet, I stumbled over something. Lowering myself to the floor, I felt around in an attempt to determine what exactly it was that had made me trip.

Feeling the object, I found the answer to my questions. Bodies; two to be exact. Although I couldn't say for sure, but in the darkness they appeared to be huddled together, and they were cold.

Taking a moment for reflection, I gathered my thoughts, rose to my feet once again and continued to make my way along the wall, still looking for a way out of this entrapment that I had been dropped into. Another half-dozen steps and I struck gold. My left hand landed on what I recognized as a door. With little effort, I found the location of the doorknob. One problem, it was missing.

Along the other edge of the door casing my hand landed on a light switch. An instant later the room was illuminated and realized that the number of dead bodies was actually five.

In disbelief, I sank to the floor, leaned against the door and began to contemplate my growing dilemma. "What the hell have you gotten me involved in, Doctor Winters?"

My mind drew a blank, but that wasn't about to stop me. Not satisfied with the status quo of my situation, I made my way back to the couple that I had just tripped over. Their bodies were cold, but not yet decayed. A man and woman, cuddled together with no outward signs of foul-play. I figured that their deaths were fairly recent, maybe a day or so at most.

That could not be said for the next victim. I think that this body was that of a woman, whose putrid corpse had been there for a long time.

The other two appeared to be men. Their bodies were in two different advanced stages of decay. One with fly larvae crawling from every orifice, and the other with his flesh the consistency of gelatin.

It became evident that the doctor's friend was a busy man with one thing on his mind; murder, for murder's sake.

My sixth sense told me that my roommates most likely arrived at this death room in much the same way I had. After a quick examination of the two bodies that were still intact, I thought that their demise was probably not due to trauma, but rather a result of prolonged dehydration and starvation.

I was well aware of the fact that people can live without food for weeks. I also knew that people can only last a few days without water. That fact alone was making me more thirsty. The last time I had anything to drink was sometime before I answered the door to find Doctor Winters standing there.

It didn't take long before I began to feel as though my mouth was void of any saliva at all. Try as I may, I couldn't help but realize that without water from somewhere, that in two or three more days I would become the sixth victim in this room.

Making my way to one of the four corners of this death room I slid my back down the wall until I found myself in a sitting position with my legs outstretched. Unable to see a way out of my current predicament, I closed my eyes and tried to rest in an attempt to conserve what energy I had left.

To be quite honest, I had no idea how long I was in this corner, but when I opened my eyes, I found myself staring up at what appeared to be a water pipe running across the ceiling. Directly above me was a valve followed by an elbow which directed the pipe upward into the ceiling. The fact that there was, in all likelihood, a room above me and that I was most likely being held in a basement didn't matter to me. What I was more interested in was the size of the pipe and the design of the water valve. From what I could tell from my vantage point, it was a half-inch copper pipe with a valve located in the middle, that contained a drain cap built into the side of its body.

I wasn't a plumber by any stretch of the imagination but I knew enough to recognize a domestic water pipe when I saw one. I also knew enough that if I was able to shut the valve off, remove the drain cap, open the valve slightly, I'd have a supply of drinking water.

The elixir of life was, from what I estimated, a mere nine feet above the floor where I was sitting. Once on my feet, I extended my arm upward. My outstretched hand was still a foot and a half from the valve.

Returning to my spot on the floor, I leaned back into the corner and once again closed my eyes. This time I wondered if the poor souls who lay dead in the room just a few feet from where I now sat, also knew that their life-saving salvation was just above them.

When I opened my eyes, I looked over at the bodies of the man and woman, who in the final moments of life chose to hold one another in an attempt to find comfort in death.

A couple of minutes later, I was on my feet again. My thirst was now replaced by my quest for life.

I walked the few steps to where the couple lay. Looking down at them, I said out loud, "I know that you can't hear me, but allow me to introduce myself. I'm Professor Buckley Doyle." I knew that they wouldn't be speaking back to me, but I continued with, "Trust me when I tell you that I mean no disrespect, but I need your help."

After taking a deep breath, I bent down, separated their bodies from one another and then dragged the man to his new spot. After stretching the man's body flat on the floor, I retrieved the women's body and placed her directly on top of her dead companion.

With a cringe, I looked down at the couple and said, "I'm so very sorry about this."

A second later I stepped up onto their bodies, stretched my arms skyward and turned the handle on the valve that was attached to the ceiling. Satisfied that the valve was in the off position, I placed my thumb and index finger on the small drain cap. Squeezing as tight as I could, I attempted to remove it but it didn't budge.

On my second try the woman's body gave way causing me to slip and fall to the floor, my head landing on the poor thing's collapsed chest cavity. When my eyes refocused, I found myself face-to-face with what remained of a once beautiful woman. In disgust of my actions, I closed my eyes and rolled to the side of the stacked bodies. For a moment I forgot about just how thirsty I was and as I gazed up at the ceiling, I asked for their forgiveness.

CHAPTER III

I wasn't exactly sure how much time had passed, but it seemed like an eternity. With my need for water escalating I soon became unable to concentrate on finding a way out of what I hoped would not become my personal death room as well.

I now lay there focusing only on the dead bodies lying beside me, the image of the woman's face beginning to permanently etch itself into my mind.

What was first an occasional closing of my eyes was now becoming increasingly frequent and the duration of my mind-easing darkness became comforting.

Eventually I found myself fantasizing only on my own mortality. Times when I thought that I was coherent, I would ask the couple next to me questions about who they were and why were they here. I couldn't understand why they wouldn't answer me, but I kept asking.

I had all but given up and fell into my own circle of darkness until I heard a man's voice telling me to come back, "Buckley, Buckley, wake up Buck." I felt his hand on my face and heard him utter, "Call 911."

In the background I could faintly hear a woman say, "It's both a medical and police emergency."

The next thing I knew, I was in a wash of illumination as a white cloud engulfed me. Everyone in the death room was standing and looking down on me. As I rose to their level, the man that I had been lying next to, was now poking at my arm with a sharp object and his woman companion was placing something over my face in an attempt to smother me. In the distance I could hear the familiar sweetness of a woman's voice repeating my name.

I could see my mother looking down at me now, and I replied, "Mom, is that you, Mom?"

In reply, the woman answered, "No Buckley, it's me, Elizabeth. Both John and I are here with you now, dear."

The man's voice added, "You're going to be all right, Buck."

Questioning my own presence, I mumbled, "Why have you both joined me? Did Winters kill you too?"

I could hear my mother's voice ask, "What did he say?"

I asked, "Why are you here?"

"It's me, Buckley. It's Elizabeth."

The next thing I knew, I was lying on the floor in the death room. I couldn't move, was very confused and unable to comprehend how all the dead people were now alive. Things were peaceful, I was relaxed and everyone around me was so very nice. I closed my eyes and when I reopened them, things seemed better.

As reality began to return, I realized that I had been hallucinating. Slightly more coherent, I moved my oxygen mask to the side of my face and said, "What about the others? Is anyone taking care of the others?"

John bent closer and answered my concerns with, "First responders are taking care of the others."

"There are five of them, John. They're all dead."

"I know, Buck. I know."

Liz leaned forward, kissed me on my forehead and whispered, "I love you, Buckley."

Straightening up, she added, "Thank God we found you when we did."

Feeling stronger, mostly because of IV hydration, I asked, "How did you find me?"

"Your grad student..."

"Annie?"

"Yes, I believe that's her name. She called me, and said that you were a no-show for your morning lecture, and wanted to know if we knew where you were."

John chimed in with, "Three days later, we reported you missing."

"I was here for three days?"

"Actually, you were missing for five days before Liz was visited by a man who she recognized as that Winters fellow from Antonio's last week."

Liz said, "I was at your house looking for clues as to your whereabouts, when Winters knocked on your front door and asked for you. When I told him you'd been missing for nearly a week, he turned pale and without saying another word, turned and left. His reaction was strange, to say the least, so I followed him here."

"And where is here?"

Liz replied, "The North end of Providence. From all that we've gathered, it appears to be Doctor Winters son's house. I called John and then I heard gunshots, so I called Detective Callahan."

"I'm pretty sure Winters' son paid me a visit right after his father did. Winters asked for help preventing a murder. I told him to contact the police. Perhaps I should have listened to him."

A familiar gruff voice replied, "Perhaps he should have taken your advice." Callahan walked around so that I could see him and added, "We found the Doctor's body upstairs next to that of, who we believe to be, his son's. An apparent murder-suicide."

Looking up at Callahan, I said, "I'm curious as to who killed who?"

"It's appears that Doctor Winters killed his son and then took his own life."

"That makes me feel worse than I already do."

John placed his hand on my shoulder and tried to ease my guilt, "There's nothing you could have done to prevent this from happening, Buck."

Not saying a word, Liz placed her hand on top of her husband's and gave it a little squeeze.

"It's a bit premature, but all the evidence points to the fact that the younger Winters was a serial killer. You're damn lucky you're still alive, Professor."

With that piece of wisdom conveyed, Callahan turned and walked away.

THE END

A
PACKAGE
AT
THE DOOR

Annie and I left my house and walked to the East Side Cafe for an early breakfast. We had spent much of last evening reviewing parts of her dissertation which she would be presenting at the end of the month. Even though her work had undergone more than its share of editing, she wanted to make sure that she had dotted all the i's and crossed all the t's. After all, it's crunch time and she knew that once the documents were submitted there was no going back.

Being that it was a Saturday, we both had plenty of time to kill. While savoring our second cup of coffee, we just sat and talked. Mostly, she talked and I listened. When we finished, the two of us headed back to 928 Benefit Street to pick up from where we had left off last night.

As we left the cafe, Annie reached over and gently grabbed my hand. I pulled her close to my side as we continued to make our way down the sidewalk together.

Neither of us spoke, but rather spent our leisurely stroll enjoying the crisp winter air and the solitude of our own thoughts.

About halfway up Benefit Street, light wisps of snow began to fill the air and I could sense that a storm would soon be upon us. I slid Annie's hand into my jacket pocket, wrapped my arm around her waist and pulled her body closer to mine. By the look in her eyes, I could tell she was pleased and so was I.

The snow had intensified during our walk back and the sparse grassy areas along the way were beginning to turn a glistening white. As we approached my house I could see a package sitting on my doorstep. Like the grass and the two of us, it too was dusted in a shimmer of light snow.

As I unlocked the front door, Annie bent down and picked up the package. After brushing the snow away, she asked, "Were you expecting a package from…" She wiped the label clear one more time and continued reading, "from someone in River Junction, Pennsylvania?"

I opened the door and motioned for Annie to go inside. As I followed her in, I replied, "I was just in River Junction a couple of months ago. I forgot my hat at the motel, but no, I wasn't expecting to ever see it again." Appreciative that a thoughtful desk manager sent it to me, I looked at Annie and said, "Just set it by the door. I'll open it later."

As Annie headed upstairs to get a towel to dry her hair, I hung our jackets on the hall tree and headed to my library to start a fire.

I futzed around with the fireplace for a while until Annie returned. With her body halfway through the door, she said, "I'm making myself a cup of tea, would you like one?"

A moment of hesitation fell over me as I found myself enamored by her partial silhouette as it appeared framed in the doorway. I locked that vision in my mind replying, "Yes, please."

With a quick smile, she disappeared back into the kitchen and I went back to poking at the logs in the fireplace.

Annie returned to the warmth of the library with two steaming cups of tea. She placed one on the table next to my chair and set the other cup on the old chest that I substituted for a coffee table. Before I had a chance to say, 'thank you' she said, "I'll get your package so you can open it."

I blew over the top of my cup, took a sip and said, "I'll get a knife."

172

From the hall, she replied, "Don't have to, I already have one."

"Not surprised."

"I heard that."

I raised my eyebrows, smelled and took a sip of my tea.

Annie returned with the package and said, "Sit next to me so we can open it together."

"It's just an old baseball hat, you can open it."

"It's not about opening a box, It's about you sitting next to me on the couch."

With cup in hand, I made my way to her side.

Annie nudged closer, placed the cardboard box on our laps, held up her pocket knife and said, "Okay, let's open her up."

After slitting inordinate amounts of packaging tape, Annie folded back the flaps and said, "Peanuts, I hate these little green things."

"I'm sure there's more than just filler in there. Didn't you ever have Cracker Jacks when you were a kid?" I smiled and added, "You need to feel around inside before you find the surprise."

Fishing around in the box, Annie abruptly stopped and removed her hand. She slid the box from her lap onto mine, then stood up. Taking two backward steps away from the couch and with her hands in the air, she said, "I think you should call the police."

Surprised by her reaction, I looked up at Annie and questioned, "What could possibly be inside this box that would warrant calling the police?"

Annie retreated all the way back to my easy chair, sat down, tucked her feet under her and sat on her hands. Before I had a chance to ask her what was going on, she said, "Believe me when I tell you; you need to call the police."

"Really?"

With an urgency in her voice, she said, "Go ahead, look for yourself."

I reached in amongst the static-charged green peanuts and pulled out a human bone.

I could hear Annie gasp as I held the object up to the light for a more in-depth look.

After a few moments I looked over at Annie, and said, "It's a rib, a human rib, that much I can tell you." I held it up to the light again, and then added, "Based on the size, and the fact that it's spongy looking without being totally fused, I'd say it is most likely from a child."

Annie pursed her lips, then asked, "Is it real?"

"Oh yah, it's real all right." As I rotated the bone around in my fingers for a better look, I had a feeling that I knew exactly who the child was that once possessed this rib within her young body. Keeping that information to myself, for now anyway, I merely added, "Whoever this child is I'd guess that they died around twenty to twenty-five years ago."

"Now can we call the police?"

"I'm not quite ready just yet."

"Why?"

"I need to know who sent it. More importantly, I need to know why they sent it."

"That's why we have police, you know. Call your friend Detective Callahan."

I smiled and replied, "He's a homicide cop."

174

"Exactly."

"I don't want to get him involved."

"That's what he does for a living."

"I need to do a little investigating myself first."

Annie freed her hands and legs from her self-imposed entanglement, stood up and walked away. She was half way to the kitchen when she looked back and said, "Is this going to be one of those, 'I'm a detective things', the ones where you're not going to tell me what's going on because you always think you can solve it better than anyone else, things?" She paused and then added, "Because if it is, I'll just head back to my apartment and you can stay here by yourself and play detective to your hearts content all by yourself."

I didn't comment because I didn't have a suitable answer to give her.

Sensing that I was paying no attention to her, Annie said, "I'll just get my things and leave."

While Annie was upstairs gathering her belongings, I added another log to the fire, then pulled back the curtains on the doors that provided privacy from the outside deck. To my surprise, what had started as a flurry when we were walking back from the cafe, was now close to a foot deep.

I walked upstairs to the bedroom, placed my hands on Annie's shoulders and gently turned her to face me. Looking into her eyes, I said, "I'm sorry if I upset you, I'll call Detective Callahan first thing on Monday."

Turning slightly toward the window, Annie replied, "It's still snowing out, you know."

We spent much of what was left of our afternoon upstairs.

It was starting to get dark outside by the time the two of us made our way back to the first floor.

I turned on the outside lights and looked out onto the deck. The snow glistened in the glow of the spotlights and had drifted halfway up the rail. I left the lights on, the curtain drawn and made my way over to the fireplace where a few embers had remained glowing. I laid a couple of well split logs across the andirons, crumpled up a few pages of yesterday's Journal, shoved them underneath and gave the whole thing a few pokes. I stood there for a minute or two watching as the fire stated to roar and then I plopped down into my favorite chair.

When Annie joined me, I poured each of us a glass of wine, and suggestively commented, "You do know that's it's brutal out there, right?"

Annie took a sip of her wine as she looked out at the deck. When the lights flickered and then went out, she turned to face me and replied, "Maybe I should spend another night."

Despite her company, I didn't sleep well and was out of bed and downstairs by three in the morning. The power was back on, so I boiled a kettle of water and brewed myself a mug of tea.

Turning off the kitchen lights, I made my way to the library and got the fire going again. With the only light in the room coming from the fireplace, I took a sip of my tea, picked up the small bone before me and gazed at it as the flames danced in the background.

I had no forensic proof, but I knew in my heart whose body this bone once occupied.

What I didn't know was why someone would send this bone to me. What's even more puzzling is the fact that after all these years some individual made a conscious decision to part with it.

It was much too early in the morning to call anyone and to start asking questions. So I sent Liz a text instead. "Liz, Did you send me a package yesterday?"

"Buckley, It's 4:00 a.m. But to answer your question, NO!"

I leaned back into my chair, stared into the fire and fell into intense thought.

Liz is a good friend. She's also the wife of my best friend, John Cooper. I'd give my life to protect either of them.

I believe Liz was truthful with her answer. However, the fact remains; whether she realizes it or not, she's clearly involved and is in way over her head.

The bottom line is, someone sent me this old rib bone from a young child and that person knows the real truth about Liz's past.

My curious nature for digging for details may very well lead to knowledge that could threaten to expose her past. The fact is that Liz's current life started when she assumed the identity of a deceased eight-year-old child and made it her own. Young Elizabeth Beck died an innocent child and was reincarnated twenty years later as the woman we know today as Liz Cooper.

The sun had not yet risen, and I found myself still sitting alone in front of a dwindling fire. It was a snowy Sunday morning with a lot of unanswered questions floating around in my mind.

Exactly who was Liz before she became Elizabeth Beck, the adult? Why all the secrecy surrounding her past? If Liz isn't her real name, then what is it and where did she come from?

I needed answers. Or did I?

If I continue down the path that my brain always tells me to take, I find the answers that I'm looking for. But at who's cost? If the truth ultimately hurts people I love and care deeply for, then perhaps I shouldn't go down that road.

On the other hand, if I drop it altogether I'll be left with a feeling of self-betrayal.

The truth or self-betrayal? As I sat in quiet solitude all I could do was ponder over the intersection of my own intellectual crossroad.

It was still dark outside when I wrapped the bone in a linen napkin, placed it in the hidden draw of my secretary and, for the time being, locked it away.

The sun was up and the sky was blue by the time Annie came downstairs. I gave her a good-morning kiss, then told her that I had called Callahan earlier, that he stopped by to pick up the bone and was going to deliver it to the coroners office for analysis.

I lied, and I felt like crap afterward.

THE END

Thank you for reading

and

I hope you enjoyed

THE DIAGNOSIS

and other

Buckley Doyle

Short Stories

THANK YOU

Robert Donnelly

Novels by Robert Donnelly include:

Buckley Doyle Mysteries:

- IN THE NAME OF THE RAVEN
- a.k.a ELIZABETH COOPER

Sam Pierce Novels:

- FATAL SUCCESSION
- MURDER UNDER THE CRESCENT MOON
- GEORGE STREET

Robert Donnelly was born in Attleboro, Massachusetts and now resides in Harrisville, Rhode Island with his wife, Deborah.

A graduate of Roger Williams University, he worked as an Engineering Manager in manufacturing before establishing and operating his own service business. A former Green Beret, he uses his military and travel experiences as background information for his writing.

Made in United States
North Haven, CT
03 July 2025

70317928R00111